THE PROPHECY OF THE DRAGONIX

DENISE RODDIS

Editor: Lesley Jones – Perfect the Word
Cover designer: Fantasy Book Design
Book formatting: Istvan Szabo, Ifj. – Fiverr/Sapphire Guardian Intl.
Printed in Great Britain by Charlesworth Press

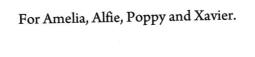

For Amelia, Alfie, Poppy and Xavier.

Contents

Chapter 1
The Beginning

It was 17.56 when the knock came at the door. Up until this point, Mrs Raleigh had been pacing the kitchen intermittently, picking items up only to put them back down again in exactly the same place. Her fussy actions were those of a worried mother. She was not sure whether she had done the right thing, but she convinced herself that in light of the timescale that had passed, her phone call was completely justified, as opposed to completely nonsensical. Clock watching, she sprayed disinfectant liberally on the varnished wooden work surface and wiped away the residue with a thin yellow disposable cloth she had located in the cupboard below the stainless-steel sink. Mrs Raleigh then fussed with one last item in the kitchen – the kettle – now positioned centrally on its blue cast-iron stand, with the handle neatly set to the right. Finally, having wiped her hands dry down the side of her skirt, she hastened to open the cottage door.

'Good afternoon. I'm Inspector Waghorn and this is PC Tullen.' Mrs Raleigh looked at the uniformed gentleman. He had a pleasant face and was clean-shaven with a jutting jawline. He appeared to be in his late forties, of medium build, with short mousey brown hair slightly receding at the temples. His colleague, a young attractive woman ten years or so his junior, had yellow-blonde hair tied neatly back in a bun. She was the smiley one of the two and Mrs Raleigh thought it was clear she was new to the job.

'Hello, er … please come in,' said Mrs Raleigh, feeling emotionally displaced. Dudley, in the meanwhile, had taken advantage of Mrs Raleigh's preoccupied focus and, on hearing voices, diverted his attention from chewing her dressing gown to running downstairs to greet the new arrivals. Amidst a frenzy of puppy excitement, involving Dudley jumping frantically up and down at both police officers' legs and much dog-related questioning on both police officers' parts, Mrs Raleigh grabbed a hold of Dudley's collar and led him to his crate.

The holiday cottage the police had entered was quaint, to say the least. The flint and cement exterior added to its charm. It was small yet cosy. The front door opened into a tiny entrance area and an internal door with a wooden lower panel and glass upper revealed the sitting area. Mrs Raleigh noticed how both Inspector Waghorn and PC Tullen hesitated to walk on the tightly woven neutral woollen carpet with their shoes on. She invited both police officers to take a seat. She observed Inspector Waghorn's approving nod as he walked across to the Bergère burgundy tartan chair. He placed a hand on either armrest and, once seated, shuffled himself snugly into the backrest. PC Tullen had made her way to the two-seater neutral sofa opposite the door. She adjusted one of the three square red, white and black striped cushions before making herself comfortable. Mrs Raleigh had thought how well-considered the entire layout of the holiday cottage was when she arrived the previous day. No attention to detail was spared. The kitchen area was equally well equipped; it contained everything from an electric whisk to a garlic crusher – she prided her-

3

self on her homemade spaghetti bolognese, complete with not one, but two garlic cloves. Her recipe was a firm family favourite and there was always excitement around who would handle the garlic crushing gadget. Before she took her seat, feeling a little shivery, she flicked the switch of the remarkably convincing imitation coal-effect electric heater, which was positioned in a recess where once a blazing open fire would have warmed the entire cottage.

'So, you're on holiday? When exactly did you arrive in Tuckenhay?'

'Yesterday,' said Mrs Raleigh. She thought for a moment as Inspector Waghorn wrote down her one-word response. PC Tullen looked at her notepad with a supportive nod of her head, which encouraged Mrs Raleigh to provide a little more information. 'Err ... yes, it was quite a journey. We've not been to Tuckenhay before. The children were so excited at the prospect of exploring. They were delighted with their rooms.'

'We would like to look in the rooms later if that's okay?' said Inspector Waghorn.

Mrs Raleigh nodded her approval and continued. 'We went for a brief walk around the facilities last night.' She paused while Inspector Waghorn scribbled quickly in an attempt to keep up now. PC Tullen met eyes with Mrs Raleigh as if to reassure her that she was doing very well. Mrs Raleigh lost focus momentarily as she wondered whether PCs were trained in reassuring glances. As she regained her focus there was a brief interruption from Inspector Waghorn's handheld transceiver. A muffled voice provided what may have been some important information but, in the circumstances, Mrs Raleigh failed to absorb the dialogue that was taking place. What was being said appeared to be of no importance to Inspector Waghorn because, without glancing up, he gripped the transceiver and pressed a button to the side, cutting the dialogue off. Mrs Raleigh was not entirely sure as to the purpose of this action because further interruptions continued to occur during the interview. She wondered why the inspector just did not turn off the transceiver completely; that, or at least answer the caller. With the continuing interruptions, she just decided to follow Inspector Waghorn's example and take no notice either.

'So, you were saying, children – these are the two you reported missing?' said Inspector Waghorn.

'Yes,' said Mrs Raleigh. 'My daughter Poppy and her friend Jay.' Mrs Raleigh knew the next lot of information she was about to provide would be detailed so rather than talk randomly, she awaited direction from Inspector Waghorn.

'Ok, can we start with your daughter Poppy – can you describe her?' asked Inspector Waghorn. PC Tullen provided another reassuring glance.

'Yes,' said Mrs Raleigh, starting to feel emotional as tears welled up in her eyes. She had never had to describe her daughter in such precise detail until this point. The thought of Poppy's beautiful thick, blonde, chest-length wavy hair and cheeky smile that she took for granted each day suddenly brought home the reality of the situation. The magnitude of emotions and thoughts attached to the whereabouts of her missing daughter and her daughter's friend Jay was beginning to impact upon her. PC Tullen offered Mrs Raleigh a tissue from a handy pack in her jacket.

Mrs Raleigh smiled gently as she reached across to receive the tissue graciously. With a nod and a thank you, she continued to answer Inspector Waghorn's questions.

'Can I have Poppy's date of birth?' asked Inspector Waghorn.

'Yes, the second of December, 2005.' Mrs Raleigh sensed Inspector Waghorn beginning to compute so to save precious time, added swiftly, 'She's thirteen.'

'Can you give me her height and build and tell me what she was wearing when you last saw her?'

'She's around 153 centimetres tall, weighs approximately forty-five kilos, is of petite build and she was wearing grey denim jeans with a short white ribbed T-shirt. She was wearing an open shirt as well, if you know what I mean.' PC Tullen nodded to confirm she knew exactly what Mrs Raleigh meant. Mrs Raleigh went on, 'She was also wearing white trainer socks and some grey and white designer trainers. Her hair was tied up in a high ponytail.'

'Is she quite a happy young lady in general? What sort of things is she interested in?' PC Tullen asked.

'Yes, she's a happy girl. She's chatty, bubbly, quite a bright girl academically.' Mrs Raleigh controlled her emotions. 'She loves performing, singing and dancing. She often posts videos of herself.'

'So, a confident young lady? And who would she post these videos to?' asked Inspector Waghorn – another double question.

'Oh, not terribly confident,' Mrs Raleigh replied quickly, keen to eradicate any misrepresentations or misconceptions. 'She only posts videos to her friends, you know, she has one of those apps,' she continued quickly. 'She's very good with "stranger danger" and all that sort of thing. My husband and I talk to her about being careful. She's exposed to internet safety all the time in her computing lessons at school, so there are no issues there.' There was a pause as Mrs Raleigh stopped to compose herself, ready to relay more information and to allow Inspector Waghorn to take down the particulars. 'She loves horses and has her own pony. Oh ... and she's good at sport. Very good – she's always selected for school matches. She plays netball, rounders and hockey – particularly hockey. In fact, she's a member of a hockey club and has progressed really well. She's been selected for different teams including playing for her county. She's quite a tenacious player. Although petite, she has a real presence on the field. A player you can rely on.' Mrs Raleigh talked with pace as the account of her daughter's profile poured from her mouth. She was not sure whether any of this information was of benefit, but she felt it appropriate to portray her daughter's positive character fully. 'She's respected by her team and popular amongst her friends. She has energy and passion and her dad's quick wit and sense of humour.' Mrs Raleigh paused. It was quite a creditable list and by no means exhaustive, which left her momentarily feeling proud.

'She sounds quite a talented young lady – you must be proud,' PC Tullen said.

'And Mr Raleigh is …?' said Inspector Waghorn.

'He's away in London. He's an architect working on a commercial project,' Mrs Raleigh said. 'He's aware of the situation, of course. I'm keeping him updated and I'll call him again once you've left. If Poppy and Jay don't turn up in the next hour or so and this looks … well, you know what I mean, he'll be here. This could all end up being something of nothing.'

'Absolutely,' said Inspector Waghorn. Mrs Raleigh was not sure whether the tone of Inspector Waghorn's one-word response should be taken as reassurance that the children would return or was he just trying to appease her? Inspector Waghorn adjusted himself slightly in the chair; tapping the ball of his right foot twice on the floor, he edged forward and glanced briefly at Mrs Raleigh, then with note-pad and pencil poised he returned his focus to his notepad. 'Now,' he checked back through previous pages of his notepad, 'it's Jay, isn't it? Can you describe him?'

'Yes,' said Mrs Raleigh. 'Jay's a tall boy. He's around 160 centimetres. Long legs. He's black, has very short cropped hair, medium build, he's quite a strong boy. Very sporty too. Very good at high jump, rugby and football. He's a very polite young man.'

Mrs Raleigh noted how Inspector Waghorn's left eyebrow dipped as he tapped his pencil twice on his notepad.

He had an inquisitive look upon his face and seemed to be collecting his thoughts. She wished she could read his mind. What was he thinking? An uneasy feeling stirred within her stomach. She became distracted. Oh dear. What was she thinking of? This was an unfamiliar place. Was there something she could have done better? Had she been in some way irresponsible? No – she convinced herself. This situation could happen to anyone. 'So, how long have Poppy and Jay been friends?'

'Oh gosh, since they started South Mount Preparatory School,' said Mrs Raleigh. 'I can remember it clearly now, Reception Class. Jay was playing with the waterwheel. Poppy went across to join in what he was doing, and they've been inseparable ever since. Oh, don't get me wrong, Jay has his boy friends he hangs out with and Poppy spends time with her girlfriends, but he and Poppy have so much in common. They enjoy each other's company.'

'Oh, so they're not sweet on each other?' said Inspector Waghorn, half smiling. Mrs Raleigh paused as her heart skipped a beat. A small pool of annoyance bubbled deep within her stomach. Where was the inspector going with this question? He had smirked also when asking it. Was it appropriate under the circumstances to lighten the mood? What on earth was he suggesting? Did he think they had romantically eloped together? A flush of irritation filled Mrs Raleigh's head and she looked at Inspector Waghorn with a furrowed brow. As she did so he adjusted his sitting position awkwardly.

'Oh no, no. The thought of being boyfriend and girlfriend would repulse them! They're best friends and everyone accepts that.'

'Okay,' said Inspector Waghorn. He asked whether the children had any contacts in the area, friends, if there was any reason for them to go off and whether either had a mobile phone with them. Mrs Raleigh responded 'no' on all counts. 'Can I check the bedrooms?' asked Inspector Waghorn.

'Yes, of course,' said Mrs Raleigh as she and both Inspector Waghorn and PC Tullen in unison pushed themselves up from their seats.

Mrs Raleigh stood by, feeling rather helpless as both police officers searched the children's rooms. Drawers were opened, mattresses and pillows lifted with seemingly no result. She was not completely sure what the two police officers were trying to find and the whole exercise seemed to bring about no clues. 'Due to the ages and the time missing, we will be putting this down as a high-risk case,' said Inspector Waghorn. 'We'll have a patrol car out looking. PC Tullen or I will keep you updated. If you need to speak to me in the meantime, if you have any further information or there are developments, do not hesitate to call me on this number.' Inspector Waghorn handed Mrs Raleigh a card. 'I'm going to leave my card with you along with an incident number that I'll write on the back. You need to quote this if you call.'

Mrs Raleigh nodded saying, 'Okay,' and 'Thank you.'

Inspector Waghorn and PC Tullen descended the tight stairs. They took position by the front door. Inspector Waghorn suddenly stopped and a curious expression crept across his face … 'Ah, there's just one more thing. When was the last time you saw the children and what were they doing?'

Chapter 2
The River

'Bagsy I get the biggest room!' said Poppy. Mrs Raleigh noticed the nudge her daughter gave Jay.

'Argh!' Her bony elbow must have hurt. The excitement was clearly all too much and the pain experienced was quickly converted to banter as Jay challenged Poppy: 'Whoever gets in first gets to choose!'

Mrs Raleigh had barely switched off the car engine before the passenger doors were flung open and both Jay and Poppy made a race for the front door of the cottage. There was laughter, intermittent shrieking and the odd shout of 'hey' on her daughter's part as both shoved each other to get nearest to the opening of the door. Mrs Raleigh closed the car door and opened the boot. She ignored both children's infuriating behaviour. She walked towards the cottage door with the key in hand. 'Well, unless you two move away from the door, I don't think either of you will get in to claim a room.'

'This is true,' said Jay, and he lifted his right index finger in jest to meet Poppy's gaze. There was a momentary silence, yet no sooner than Mrs Raleigh had turned around than the children had pushed past and made a dart for the opening. Without exploring or commenting upon the quaintness of the downstairs living area, both children ran immediately up the narrow staircase. Mrs Raleigh followed. Poppy, being of slight build, had managed to nimbly squirm under Jay's right arm as he held on to the bannister before ascending the stairs – she looked thrilled by the advantage. From the audible excitement, she had clearly found the master bedroom first. It was in keeping with a cottage theme. There was a double bed covered with a floral quilted cover and matching curtains. This room fitted Mrs Raleigh's expectations beautifully. The children in turn glanced quickly at the room, and, realising it wasn't theirs, raced along the landing barging each other. They brushed against the cream painted walls, much to Mrs Raleigh's displeasure. Poppy ran into the next room. This was smaller; there was a continuation of the leaf-green carpet, a similar quilt covering the single bed along with matching curtains. The walls this time were painted a pale apple green. There was a stained oak dressing table against the wall at the base of the bed. Poppy sat and momentarily flicked her hair while looking in the mirror before getting up and racing towards the top of the landing. There were no more bedrooms upstairs, and this was a three-bedroom cottage; an expression of realisation swept across the children's faces. 'There's another room!' Both children raced downstairs. They turned left past the bathroom and discovered the other single room. There was another dressing table, floral bedding and curtains, lilac painted walls, and a window looking out towards another holiday cottage. 'I hate lilac! I'm having the green room upstairs,' said Poppy.

'Yeah, well, I don't have to go far to the bathroom, and I've got an easy escape route if I want to go outside,' Jay said.

'So, are we all settled with room choices?' Mrs Raleigh asked.

'Yeah!' they both said.

After a lunch of sandwiches, crisps, cake and juice, Jay and Poppy were keen to get out and explore the surrounding area. Dudley the Cockapoo was busily pacing around, stopping only to offer a paw accompanied by an occasional whine; he too clearly wanted to go out. 'Right, come along then, get your shoes on. Can someone just grab those dog treats?' said Mrs Raleigh.

Mrs Raleigh stepped outside the door; she felt the sun warm on her face as she glanced up at the picturesque sky – pale blue with an occasional fluffy white stationary cloud. She walked; it was relatively peaceful, which was a welcome break from the previous excitement. All she could hear was the crunch of the gravel underneath her feet; she descended the stone steps, aware of Jay and Poppy behind her. Just to the right were the freshly marked tennis courts. She smelt the sun-scorched rubber, which was quickly superseded by the scent of chlorine from the swimming pool. The vibrant colours of the flower-filled terracotta pots on the terrace caught her attention. A gentle breeze touched her face as she glanced beyond to the wide gravel pathway that led towards the lane. Her feet sank into the springy carpet of the immaculately groomed lawn. A delightful aroma drifted from the beautifully maintained flower beds, home to a vibrant display of clematis, jasmine and honeysuckle. Simply exquisite. Situated apart on the lawn were two small white circular wrought-iron tables, each accompanied by two matching chairs. An ideal setting for afternoon tea, she thought. Beyond the lawn was a meadow – home to two white goats. A plaque attached to the gate informed passers-by that one goat was aptly named Billy, the other, Elise. Jay and Poppy spotted the animals and, raced over for a closer inspection. 'Oh my gosh!' said Poppy. 'They're weird.'

'Hey!' said Jay. 'Well that's nice. I bet they think you're weird.'

'Actually, I think they're looking at you thinking you're weird. Look at the way old Elise is eyeing you up and down.' Poppy laughed, nudging Jay in the side twice with her elbow.

'I think you'll find she's actually thinking *who's this hot dude?*' said Jay.

'Hmm … so let me get this straight. This goat, Elise, fancies you. So, you have a goat for a girlfriend … yeah, well, that'll be about right,' said Poppy.

'Oh, very funny. Well, at least I have a goat interested in me, unlike you,' Jay commented. 'Your goat is gurning his jaw as if he's disappointed with *his* choice of girlfriend!'

'Girlfriend! What are you going on about? You're weird,' said Poppy.

'What are you two up to?' asked Mrs Raleigh.

'Nothing,' said Poppy, giggling.

Smirking, Jay added, 'Admiring goats.'

'Hmm …' said Mrs Raleigh, not entirely convinced by the responses.

Having navigated the gate, everyone entered the meadow. Poppy and Jay walked on ahead, absorbing their surroundings. Dudley pulled on the lead to catch up and Mrs Raleigh attempted to control his excitement by pulling him back. In doing so she caught her right foot in a small divot. 'Oh, for goodness sake!' she said, blaming Dudley entirely for the incident which she knew deep down was her own fault for not having looked where she was going.

It was such a glorious day, bar the twisting of her ankle. The meadow was filled with sweet-smelling untamed green grass and there were cowslips and buttercups scattered around. 'Mum, I can hear water running – can we go and see where it's coming from?'

'Yes, go on.'

Mrs Raleigh was now left alone to enjoy the peaceful surroundings with Dudley. The children were out of sight, but she thought safe in the relatively enclosed area. They could easily climb over the wooden fence beyond, but she felt neither child would attempt it due to the incredibly steep hill the other side, which was home to a flock of graz-ing sheep. The children had appeared wary of the goats, so she did not expect them to consider entering the paddock of sheep. She was also convinced that the children would know that going onto occupied farmland was not acceptable. She had already been informed by the landlord that there was a lovely walk along the shallow river and, having picked up on the word *shallow*, she concluded that the children were absolutely safe to go off; they were close by, and would return when it was time to go back to the cottage.

Poppy followed behind Jay. There was the source of the noise – a shallow river. She could hear a louder flow of water and was keen to explore where this was coming from. This she achieved in minutes. Just a short run along the bank edge led her to a small concrete overflow dam. The water was flowing fast, yet a thin branch was causing a slight restriction as it lodged across the stream. 'Hey, I know, how about we try to dislodge that branch?' said Jay.

'Okay,' said Poppy. She studied the ground for something heavy to throw at the branch and Jay did likewise. Both children intuitively started to scuff the ground with their feet in an attempt to release pieces of rock buried under the meadow grass. The challenge of dislodging a branch seemed to be a fun way to fill time.

'Here, let's try this,' said Jay.

Poppy had also managed to dislodge a sizable piece of rock. 'I'll go first,' she said. She drew back her elbow and then launched the rock forward; it would have been with all her might, but she started to laugh mid-throw so the rock splashed shy of the wedged branch.

'And that is why you are rubbish at shotput,' Jay said.

'Oh, do shut up,' said Poppy. 'Now let's see if you can do any better.' Jay had a look of determination on his face; he drew back his rock and paused momentarily before propelling it with precision. It hit the water with energy and force, making contact with the wedged branch. The branch shifted at one side, angling into the water current. Seconds later, the branch was released. This was met with rapturous applause and cheering from Jay. Poppy, jubilant inside, preferred not to show Jay how well he had done, so quietly praised him for his achievement with a thumbs up. They stood peacefully still for a moment as they watched the branch float away. There was something liberating yet calming and therapeutic about watching a lone branch moving freely. The serene feeling soon ended as the branch caught loosely on one of several roots of a large, grand-looking tree. 'Oh no,' said Poppy.

'Don't worry,' said Jay. 'I can dislodge it from the bank.'

With a purposeful stride in their step, both headed towards the tree. Upon reaching it, Jay climbed down using the roots to secure his footing and grip. A direct nudge with his right foot soon sent the branch on its way. With the mission accomplished, Poppy focused her attention to the tree roots. 'These are weird.'

'Everything's weird to you,' Jay said. 'Goats, trees.'

'No, look … well, not weird but artistic! How they … what's the word? Intertwine?' said Poppy. She was mightily impressed as she had no notion how such a creative word had entered her head.

'Yeah, if you're into all that artistic stuff,' said Jay, sounding uninterested and dismissive.

Poppy felt that her observation was valid. She studied how the tree roots curved and intertwined like a beautiful piece of Celtic lattice work. She marvelled at the sense of regularity to the very structure. It was like nothing she had ever seen before.

'This, on the other hand, is art,' said Jay, pointing out a carved hollow area in the bank behind the root structure. 'How about we sit in there?'

Both manoeuvred their way around and between the tree roots to sit cosily in what appeared to be a purpose-made alcove. They talked for a while, reminiscing about school and recent events. Poppy reminded Jay about the time when Charlotte Motley, who was in their year group, had got up in the night on a camping trip, misplaced her footing and ended up falling into the side of their Forest School Leader Mr Brown's tent – she fell on him waking him up in the process.

Poppy finally stopped talking, expecting laughter or at the very least, a comment from Jay. She heard nothing. Puzzled by the lack of response, she turned her head round to look over her shoulder. She was utterly astonished. Jay was not there … he had completely disappeared …

Chapter 3
Nutash

Poppy could see a light source on the ground towards the back of the alcove. In one swift manoeuvre she had shuffled back and rotated onto her hands and knees in an attempt to find where Jay had gone. She stopped to think for a moment. Jay absolutely did not exit the alcove in front of her – she would have noticed, surely. The light source was from a beam that shone up from the earthy floor towards the ceiling of the alcove. There was a pile of loose dirt. This must have been where he had gone through. Curiosity beckoned her to investigate further.

Having squeezed her way through the loose dirt and debris she surfaced. Her immediate reaction was to brush the soil from both her clothing and hair. At first glance, there was no sign of Jay. This Poppy perceived as strange. She felt Jay would not have wandered far without her. There was then a succession of oddities that caused her to be rather concerned. In front was a stretch of grass; beyond this point was possibly a valley, Poppy thought, as the landscape seemed to suddenly dip. There were hills beyond the valley. To her right was a dense wooded area. The tree trunks, she noted, were of a spiral formation and the branches twisted in a similar way to the peculiar-looking roots of the grand tree that guarded the entrance to the riverbank alcove. Poppy remembered thinking that she had never seen trees like that and, while she knew several tree types and could name them, she could not determine what species of trees made up this vast wood. She had never seen anything like them before. Not one hundred metres in front, slightly to the left of where she was standing, stood a quaint cottage. It was made of grey stone with a thatched roof and a picket fence around the garden. She observed what appeared to be some colourful vegetable plants, completely different from any root vegetables she had seen in her grandfather's garden. She decided that the cottage must be occupied because smoke was pouring out from the chimney. The smoke was aqua green in colour – something she had never seen before.

While there was nothing to overtly scare her, Poppy was in unfamiliar territory. The odd landscape, peculiar-looking trees, vegetables, and strange-coloured smoke pouring from the cottage chimney contributed to an unnerving, curious sensation that crept up through her body. She took a few strides forward before breaking into a jog, then back to a walk. She halted when she reached the cottage. 'Jay! Jay!' she shouted. There was no reply. Where on earth was he? He couldn't have gone far, surely? A feeling of helplessness and vulnerability now joined the unnerving sensation she was experiencing. 'Jaaaaay!' Poppy shouted as loudly as she possibly could. He must have heard her call that time, and then at least she would not have to explore the unknown surroundings to find him.

'Shh, don't shout!' said a slightly high-pitched, shrill voice. Poppy turned sharply in the direction of the speaker.

A small elderly man was beckoning her, or at least she thought he was. Having glanced briefly around there was no one else he could have been calling to. 'Shh, quick!' he called in what appeared to be an agitated manner. Poppy came to the rapid conclusion she was in some form of danger. Jay had disappeared and the only option to gain answers to her questions was possibly staring her in the face – in the form of an odd little man. She hastened over; as she did so, she was acutely aware of an equally peculiar-looking woman standing inside the cottage doorway. The little woman beckoned Poppy in with a similar level of urgency. As Poppy got closer, she noted that both the little man and the woman were not much taller than herself. They did not look human; they were elfin in appearance with pointy ears, small features and a little nose turned up slightly at the end. The male had a small speckling of brown, greying freckles across his nose and cheeks; he had a long snow-white beard shaped to a point. The little woman, somewhat younger, had similar dainty ears and turned-up nose. The little old man wore dungarees of a dark blue shade and a beige shirt underneath. The stitching was obvious on his entire outfit and Poppy presumed that the elderly couple's clothes were homemade as opposed to shop-bought. Everything Poppy understood about 'stranger danger' from what she had been told at home entered her mind. She had, however, concluded that she was far from home; in fact, it appeared in a completely different land. What Poppy perceived to be the norm in her world was not reflected in this one.

She was swiftly guided into the cottage by the elderly couple. The woman closed the wooden door behind her and pulled down the latch. 'You are safe now, I think,' she said, sounding relieved. She breathed a heavy sigh. Poppy was aware of her own breathing. It had deepened due to the boost of adrenaline initiated by the events of the last few minutes. 'What is your name? Are you from the other world?' the little woman asked.

'What do you mean? What other world? I'm Poppy, my name is Poppy and … I don't know!' Poppy was not sure whether she was confused or not, having pieced together clues affirming she was no longer in 'her' world. She became briefly aware of her surroundings during the conversation. She stood in a darkened room, the shutters were closed. It was a kitchen, with what looked like oak wooden cupboards. Her hand was gripping the back of a wooden chair. Poppy glanced down. The chair was beautifully carved, especially the backrest. It was a framework of swirls and Poppy traced the outline with her fingertips. The chair was one of four placed around a wooden table equally delicate in design. There was an open fire. She watched as the flames danced and glowed within the grate. The smoke rising from the burning wood was an aqua green colour, the colour she had observed from outside, and there was a soothing medicinal smell to whatever was burning. She no longer felt so worried. Any anxiety she was feeling slowly drifted away. She believed the elderly couple were genuinely concerned about her well-being and appeared to have her best interests at heart. They were surely friend as opposed to foe. Poppy was apparently far from home, and this couple were all she had. They were the only beings that could answer the questions at the forefront of her mind. She asked, 'Where am I? And where is my friend Jay?' The little elderly woman diverted her gaze. Poppy was acutely aware of this but nevertheless she continued to fix her attention on the little woman for an answer to her question.

'Nutash. You are in Nutash,' the woman replied, still somewhat distracted with her focus. 'My name, dearie, is Aviv and this,' she gestured towards the little old man, 'is Ashen, my ever-tied.' Poppy decided that meant they were married.

Ashen looked away also. Poppy sensed that something was happening behind her. She remained in her position. Previously a door had creaked, but she had paid little attention to the noise. She felt an increase in warmth in the room as pinkie-violet dust particles floated gracefully through the air around her. She stood motionless, wondering what could be taking place behind her. She turned her head round to the left slowly as a large strong wolf-like bear circled her. It did this a couple of times. Poppy just stood, completely stunned – paralysed momentarily by fear and by the sheer sight and size of this incredibly unusual-looking animal. As it circled, it rubbed its thick pinkie-violet body against her and then shook its coat. This action was repeated. Poppy dared not move. With its actions more particles were released from its coat which floated around the room, glistening in the threads of light that streaked through the window shutters. Some settled onto Poppy. She noted a haze of pinkie-violet mist around her body. It was as if she was surrounded by a strange translucent aura, which settled and dissipated.

'Ashen ...' said Aviv, 'Ashen, my ... my goodness. Can you see what's happening? I can hardly believe it. Xania is ... is protecting her. She is being protected. It is her – she is the chosen one.'

Chapter 4
Tuckenhay Police Station

PC Tullen followed Inspector Waghorn out of the cottage having noted from Mrs Raleigh exactly what the children were doing before they disappeared. They didn't talk during the short walk from the cottage door to their vehicle. PC Tullen held on to the car door handle as the inspector unlocked the door.

'What are we going to do now, sir?'

'Let's just get into the car, Tullen,' said Inspector Waghorn.

'Will we go and do a brief site investigation or will that be down to Search and Rescue?' asked PC Tullen.

'No,' Inspector Waghorn answered. PC Tullen found his tone somewhat abrupt. Her superior must have realised his curt response because with a softening on the word *we*, he added, 'We will do a brief overview of the last known site the children visited in the first instance.'

'Oh … okay,' said PC Tullen. 'Then what's the situation with the media, sir?'

'Let's just see what we find first, Tullen, shall we,' Inspector Waghorn said. 'One step at a time.'

'Sir … what are we going to do?' asked PC Tullen, confused, wondering why they were both sitting in the vehicle when the meadow was directly in front of them – the meadow being the last known site that the children visited.

'Now, Tullen, we'll drive off site before conducting our search. We don't want a somewhat frantic mother curtain-peeping our every movement. If we leave the car parked here and we're too long gone, that will cause further worry. She'll be thinking about what we might have found. And if we return in too short a time, we're likely to be offering an explanation to my superior following a complaint about our lack of dedication.'

'Right you are,' said PC Tullen, having been enlightened by this ingenious psychological theory.

PC Tullen fastened her seat belt. There was little conversation en route. She noted that the inspector looked a little deep in thought, or maybe he was merely focusing on the journey. She considered the whereabouts of both children and then tried hard to distract herself by thinking about her forthcoming holiday.

Inspector Waghorn looked like he had a clear idea as to where to drive the car. He parked the vehicle in a secluded car park. PC Tullen exited the car once Inspector Waghorn had got out and walked the short distance to the meadow with him. It was a dry day with scattered clouds that allowed long uninterrupted periods of sunshine. The temperature was pleasantly warm and there was a calmness in the air – perfect conditions for searching for evidence. 'Now ... this is where you can put some of your training into practice, Tullen. What's your immediate thinking?'

'Um … to put shoe slips on, sir, and rubber gloves – to avoid cross-contamination of the area – and I need to look for any environmental changes?'

'Yes. Good, that's the idea. Right then. Let's get on with it, shall we?'

PC Tullen navigated her way around the gate with Inspector Waghorn directly behind. They walked a short distance, stopping now and again to assess the area. Each time they stopped, PC Tullen placed her pencil to her lips, pondered, then scribbled in her notebook. This would be followed by Inspector Waghorn asking, 'Have you got something?' or, 'What have you found?'

'Not much, sir,' or, 'Nothing really, sir,' were the alternate replies from PC Tullen.

PC Tullen heard running water and hastened in the direction of the river. 'Let's look over here, sir.'

'Well, it's shallow, Tullen, so there's nothing to suggest either would have fallen in and that the other went in for a rescue. I don't think we've two kids swept to the sea!'

PC Tullen agreed. 'No, sir.' She glanced across the river. 'Look, sir.'

'What, Tullen?'

'Over there, sir, the other side of the bank – that funny little alcove.'

'What about it, Tullen?' said Inspector Waghorn looking impatient.

'I can see what look like footprints in the mud, sir.'

'Well, you can see more than I can, Tullen. Are you completely sure?'

'Yes, sir,' she said, thrilled.

PC Tullen searched for an opportunity to cross the river. Inspector Waghorn followed albeit at a slower pace. Upon locating a little quaint bridge, they went over in turn.

'Just be careful not to disturb anything,' said Inspector Waghorn.

'I know, sir,' said PC Tullen. 'There's clear fresh prints,' she confirmed having reached the alcove.

'Right, take a snapshot of the tread. I'll have Bevis crossmatch with brands when we get back. Once he comes back with the results, we can confirm with the mother whether the brand matches with what the children were wearing. These kids have had a play about, done a spot of exploring and then something,' said Inspector Waghorn.

'Sir, it seems to go back and there's loose dirt.'

'Yes ... well, let's take care not to disturb the area, Tullen. I think we get the picture here, don't you?'

'It's odd, sir.'

'What's odd, Tullen?'

'The prints, sir.'

'What about the prints, Tullen?'

'I don't know, sir.'

An expression crept across Inspector Waghorn's face which suggested that PC Tullen had overly trifled with his patience. 'I think we're done here, Tullen, for the time being. Let's get back. You've got a desk to tidy, I dare say, before jetting off on your holiday tomorrow.'

PC Tullen was a little confused as to why her inspector had decided to call time on the search at a point where she felt she was on to something. 'Yes, well, I have got a couple of admin bits I need to do before going off, sir. I think my desk is tidy though.'

'I'm glad to hear it,' said the inspector.

PC Tullen and Inspector Waghorn made their way back to the vehicle. Inspector Waghorn asked several light questions, showing an interest in PC Tullen's holiday arrangements. He further provided the odd anecdote here and there during the journey back. These ranged from stories about various plane flights to hotel accommodation he had experienced. PC Tullen listened but towards the tail end of a story, her focus drifted as she gazed thoughtfully out of the window. Different thoughts flashed into her mind, but the thought of the missing children was one that remained and niggled her. Her conscious mind had noted that Inspector Waghorn had not discussed the children since the search. This did not cause her to be concerned, however, because she understood that many police officers did not wish to dwell on cases. They occupied their minds with other matters as a form of distraction. She acknowledged that as much as this was possibly good practice for mental well-being, she struggled to distract herself. It was easier advised than done. Perhaps with a few more years of incidents behind her, she might be better in the art of forgetting the things that worried or concerned her.

As another patchwork of fields passed by. PC Tullen said, 'That's it!'

'What?' said Inspector Waghorn.

'The footprints, you know, the footprints we saw in the alcove. They led down, there were some on the bank, I mean coming from the riverbank into the alcove, but then no exit prints. It's odd.'

'So, they went into the river,' Inspector Waghorn concluded.

'What? What, with their shoes on?' said PC Tullen.

'No, they took their shoes off first, Tullen, don't you think, and then jumped straight in.'

PC Tullen hesitated for a moment, just slightly miffed and considering her superior may have discredited her theory. 'Yes … but no, sir, the footprints didn't divert out towards the river. They went in towards the alcove.'

'So, as I just said, they jumped in. What are you suggesting, Tullen? They vanished into thin air?'

'No … I don't know, but they have vanished, sir, haven't they? It's just so odd. We're not talking one child here but two. This does not reek of stranger danger, it's just not a typical pattern.'

'Agreed – and this is why you have the makings of a good officer, Tullen. You're analysing, reflecting, analysing, reflecting, etcetera, using the investigative thought cycle, but I'm mindful of the fact that you are going on holiday tomorrow and you need to put yourself into a completely different mindset. I'd start now if I were you and try not to keep thinking about it. You've got a good book to read, I take it, while you're away?'

'Yes, sir – *Call of Duty*.'

'Right you are. And what might that be about, Tullen?'

'It's a police thriller, sir,' said PC Tullen.

'Now, why doesn't that surprise me?' said Inspector Waghorn with a hint of sarcasm.

PC Tullen wound her window down. She and Inspector Waghorn were moments away from Tuckenhay Police Station – a small, discreet building. It didn't really look like a police station. Not like the important looking police stations she saw on her favourite police television programmes or that had been described in the books she read. In fact, it was a bit of a disappointment; it was far removed from the Metropolitan Police Headquarters in London where two of her college friends had managed to secure jobs. The exterior was clad in local stone. The building had a thatched roof and leaded windows and it looked like a cottage. Inset into the stonework, just below the edge of the thatch, was a plaque that read 'Tuckenhay Police Station' in a deep blue font; if it were not for the plaque it would be easy to mistake the building for a private dwelling.

As she sat and reflected, she counted her blessings. When the engine stopped, she could hear birds chirping with enthusiasm in the trees, a fly buzzed passed her left ear, and there was a distant mooing. The air smelt sweet and fresh. There was no hustle and bustle here. Some days she would be lucky if she saw more than five people, and that included her colleagues. Little of any consequence had ever taken place. She reminisced about the most excitement that had occurred that year and thought about the summer fete. There were more than five people to see that day, which made it an exciting event. Homemade jams and pies arranged by the Tuckenhay's Women's Institute, the smell of sausages and burgers grilling, sweet sticky candy-floss on her lips. And there was the pink teddy she had won after managing to knock a coconut down. She could almost hear the jingling of the bells of the Tuckenhay Jolly Morris Dancers once more as they stamped their feet and wove between each other. And that was the day of the biggest drama in her career to date. The strange disappearance of dear old Grannie Annie's long-haired guinea pig, Gertie. It was discovered on the barbecue at the summer fete. PC Tullen had taken it to the local vet upon Inspector Waghorn's advice. A veterinarian autopsy concluded that Gertie had died of natural causes and had come to no harm and that the barbecue episode was a distasteful and ghastly prank. The veterinary nurse had looked at PC Tullen with a sense of suspicious interest. PC Tullen was sure it must have been her who had leaked the vet's conclusion as to

how the guinea pig died. Then there was all the parapher-
nalia of a 'whodunnit' quandary for months to follow. PC
Tullen remembered the behind-the-hand whispers as she
passed an occasional couple when walking through the
hamlet. The Reverend Joan had confided she herself was on
the list of suspects (the list that PC Tullen knew had been
compiled by several of the local residents who had nothing
much better to do with their time). She felt sorry for the
Reverend Joan; it was all because the Reverend Joan had
asked Grannie Annie, the local dressmaker, to make her a
special vestment for the Easter service. When Grannie Annie failed to finish the garment in time, whispers of a
revengeful act commenced. Common sense prevailed in
PC Tullen's mind; the Reverend Joan would not even consider harming a guinea pig, or any other animal for that
matter.

It was later brought to PC Tullen's attention that foul
play was not at the root of the death of Grannie Annie's pet
guinea pig; rather, two local schoolchildren had found Gertie motionless and cold in their back garden. Having

decided Gertie's soul had passed on, they wanted her cold body to be warm so they placed her on the barbecue.

A feeling of importance and empowerment was now building inside PC Tullen. She was finally working on something exciting. She could equal her fellows and friends in the Met with the types of cases they were involved with. Her parents would be so proud and have something to boast about at one of their dinner parties. This was what she came into policing for, and yet her moment was dashed and short-lived – she was about to go on holiday. Of all the wretched timing. The case was being left to her superior, Inspector Waghorn, who for some reason didn't seem to share the same level of enthusiasm.

Inspector Waghorn was swift to exit the car, closely followed by PC Tullen. Chief Inspector Miles had come on duty and there he was flicking through some paperwork while licking chocolate from his fingers. He was a rotund man, aged fifty, balding with silver-grey hair and a grey moustache. Today he had on a pale blue shirt with a navy tie, on the tie another noticeable egg stain. The buttons on his shirt strained from his bulging tummy.

'Guv.'

'Sir.'

'Ah, they return. Waggors, Tullen. What's been going on in merry Tuckenhay today? Or have you both been out for a sneaky cream cake? Better have brought me one back – you know I'm rather partial to a chocolate éclair.'

Inspector Waghorn quickly turned his attention to PC Tullen. 'Right, now, Tullen, get yourself off. I expect you've got much to do. I'll clear up from here – off you pop, lass.'

'But sir, don't you want me to write up my notes?' said PC Tullen, clutching her notepad.

'Notes? Goodness, no. Leave it to me,' said Inspector Waghorn eagerly as he snatched the notepad out of PC Tullen's hand. 'Right, off you go. Go on. That's the privilege of being an inspector – you get to write up notes for those going on a once-in-a-lifetime holiday! Give her a few more years and she won't be able to get out the office quick enough, eh, guv? Now if you hang around any longer I'll have you do your notes and the guv's work as well. Right, jacket, and there's your bag.' Inspector Waghorn ushered her out of the door, adding, 'I'll tell you what you can do though, you can write up a nice little postcard to keep us entertained here – we'll think of you soaking up the sunshine.'

'Oh, right, okay,' PC Tullen said.

Inspector Waghorn noted the look of confusion in Tullen's face. He had to be assertive. He didn't want her querying or questioning any more than she had already. He returned to his desk. He glanced at Chief Inspector Miles briefly to see if he was looking. He placed his hands on his desk, shuffled some papers and opened his drawer, placing PC Tullen's notepad inside, and, without saying a word, closed the drawer. He took his lanyard from his pocket while clearing his throat in an attempt to conceal any jingling of keys that might divert the chief inspector's attention towards him. He quickly fingered through the keys, covering up further jingling with two forced coughs. He located a small silver key between his thumb and forefinger, placed it swiftly into the small keyhole and locked the drawer, testing it before replacing the keys in his pocket.

'So, what's gone on today?' said Chief Inspector Miles.

'Oh, another odd disappearance,' said Inspector Waghorn, trivialising the day's event, quickly adding, 'so it's a chocolate éclair then, is it? I think I'll go with one of those too. Just what's required to finish off an odd week.' Inspector Waghorn pulled and wriggled the shirt collar from around his neck. Perspiration had formed across his forehead. He rubbed it quickly away, tapped the desk twice with both hands and breathed a sigh. His top lip was wet with perspiration; he wiped around his mouth then got up out, car keys in hand, and headed straight for the station door, not wishing to meet the chief inspector's eyes or engage in further discussion. Bother.

'Odd? There's nothing odd about disappearing animals,' said Chief Inspector Miles. A wave of relief swept over Inspector Waghorn, followed by a small ripple of guilt.

The chief inspector had assumed the 'odd' disappearance involved animals. 'People need to take better care of the pets they profess to love so much. I mean, what a waste of our time. Anybody would think we had nothing better to do.'

Inspector Waghorn continued to walk forward, his back to the chief inspector. He pretended not to hear the remark and was quietly relieved that he had not lied about the events of the day, nor, he convinced himself, had he purposely misled his superior officer.

Chapter 5
The Prophecy

'Do you know why you are here?' said Aviv.

'No ...' Poppy paused for a moment. 'I don't understand ... what do you mean *why* I'm here? I really don't know what's going on.' She took another moment to try and rationalise her thoughts. 'I was on holiday a short while ago, then my friend went missing. I tried to find him and now I'm in some ... some weird place.' Feeling she may have insulted the couple she continued, 'Sorry ... I don't mean weird, it's just strange. Jay's missing, he's my friend. I-I don't know what's happening, I was hoping you could tell me why I'm here.'

'Sit down, dearie,' Aviv said, sounding sympathetic and calm. She placed her hands on Poppy's shoulders. 'Ashen, make some saphberry brew – it will warm and refresh the poor child. She has much to know and much to do.'

Ashen went over to the stove; he heated what appeared to be water in a pan, adding the flowers and berries of a colourful spray that was lying to the side of the stove, neatly bound by a reed. Ashen stirred the brew gently and then dipped a wooden spoon into the infusion; he smelled and tasted the drink periodically. Poppy gazed on while Aviv pulled up a chair and looked at her with a curious expression. 'Once Ashen has made your brew, I will explain all you need to know,' Aviv assured her. Xania was positioned to Poppy's right, nestling to the side of her. Poppy had subconsciously reached down and found a clump of Xania's fur with her right hand and was winding this around and through her fingers slowly, which was both relaxing and comforting. It brought about a feeling of being safe. It was an action trait deeply rooted in her childhood. As a toddler at bedtime she would rub and wind her toy rabbit's ears through her fingertips. This always relaxed her before she drifted off into a gentle, deep sleep.

Xania remained by Poppy's side, also somewhat calmed by Poppy's attention.

'Xania appears to have an affinity with you,' Aviv observed.

'I like big dogs … wolves, or whatever she is,' said Poppy. Xania gave a deep-throated grumble as if disgruntled by her comment.

Ashen walked steadily across with a wooden mug in hand. Poppy could see the steam rising from it. He handed it to her carefully, instructing her to drink it slowly, taking care not to scald herself with the hot medicinal liquid. She took two initial sips. The brew was sweet at first taste with a fruity sharp aftertaste; the sharpness tingled and danced on her tongue. Then as the liquid trickled down her throat there was a soothing warmth that lingered and relaxed her with every subsequent sip. The brew was comforting and delicious, unlike anything she had tasted.

'Can I ask, what did you mean earlier about I'm protected?' Poppy asked.

'It's quite a lengthy tale I have for you, dearie. Ashen?' Aviv looked at Ashen for approval. He nodded. 'You see, there is a prophecy in Nutash. The dragonix rule the land ensuring law and order for its subjects. With each eclipsing of the New Blood Moon on the Rocky Peak, a new dragonix is born with a resealing of its egg. The dragonix is respected highly by all. It is an oracle, the font of all knowledge. It knows everything there is to know and protects its subjects from harm, all and anything. At the last eclipsing of the Blood Moon, a storm occurred of the darkest nature and, some say, a bolt of lightning so violent struck through the moon. The darkest nature *they* spoke of emerged. The egg was twinned. Zenaida rose, the new dragonix, but with her the evilest of all evils – Vasclaurus, the hideous result of the unfortunate turn of events. He was the twisted product of magic gone horribly wrong. Nutash would have continued in all its glory had Zenaida reigned supreme, but it was not to be.'

'How, what happened?' Poppy asked. Aviv went on to explain that in such a rare situation as this, the matter of the ruler had to be determined; this was outlined in the prophecy. One unbreakable pledge by each dragonix could be agreed. The first hatchling would go first. Vasclaurus, eager for control, eagerly put forth his pledge to state that he would be the ruler of all in Nutash. Zenaida realised that Nutash would now be under the merciless peril of this grotesque and demonic creature. She had to think carefully.

She had noted in her peripheral vision that two pieces of her and Vasclaurus's eggshell were being discreetly smuggled away by helpful, loyal raspins, who were clearly working for both her and Nutash. She knew what she had to say and what the consequence might be. Vasclaurus was growing impatient and there wasn't time for the removal of the third piece of eggshell. With the other two long taken, Zenaida rose tall and, with pride and bravery, conveyed her pledge. In an attempt to protect the good inhabitants of Nutash she said that upon the resealing of their eggshell pieces by a protected child from the human world, at the time of the New Blood Moon, Vasclaurus would turn to dust and, with him, all evil.

In fury, Vasclaurus towered over Zenaida. He powered down and drove his talons deep into her beating heart. She staggered back, her eyes initially transfixed, stunned from the excruciating pain; she fell backwards, but not before casting a victorious glance deep into the eyes of Vasclaurus.

'But what do you mean … you said I was the one, I am protected. What does that mean?'

'Did you not see Xania encircle you earlier and give off an aura?' said Aviv. 'You have been protected by a wolvern. A wolvern is the most sacred animal of the dragonix. Can you not see? The child from the human world – it is you. You are here to save us! But your journey is long and hard and not without fear, torment, fight and challenge. Xania can go with you but a wolvern cannot protect you in the Dark Side – that is Vasclaurus's domain. Xania can help, but not protect your life there. You must use what you know to protect you and your gifts, your strengths from the human world will be of benefit. Your skills will become more powerful and you can use them to your advantage. Your friend's skills also, but I very much fear for him unless you find him quickly. Xania will protect and help you … you are starting to build a friendship, a bond between each other. We have a saying here, that a friendship made in Nutash lives forever. But there is a further challenge other than finding the three dragonix eggshell pieces and placing them together before the Blood Moon eclipse: you must leave Nutash before the eclipse ends or you, in turn, will turn to dust.'

Chapter 6
The Dark Side

Jay felt somewhat confused. His head hurt … he had
hit a tree stump on the forest floor. It had all happened so very quickly. One minute he was crawling
out of a hole, completely perplexed as to where he was. He
had seen a quaint cottage to his right, and there was a dense
forest area with a bluey-green glowing light coming from
within it. Knowing Poppy would be hot on his heels in no
time at all, he went quickly to investigate what could be so
interesting in the wood. Upon reaching the point where the
beautiful meadowland ended and the dense forest began,
Jay thought he heard an elderly voice shout, 'Don't go in
there,' but he was too intrigued by the mystical light that he
had already stepped in.

The interesting light disappeared. Jay thought momentarily about turning back to investigate the voice, but he

was soon distracted by an eerie rustling of leaves – no other noises or movement, just the leaves on the ground swirling on their own accord. No wind to drive the force. It was strangely disturbing. Then, rising up from the depths of the ground, oily-looking black shadows began to form. More and more rose. The terrifying forms had wings and horns – they looked like grotesque evil apparitions. Jay stood pinned to the spot. He wanted to step backwards and turn and run, but it was as if his mind and body were no longer communicating with each other. The evil shadows conjoined to build a mass, an energetic force, and this force sucked at him. His legs were pulled from beneath him and his back hit the ground hard along with his head. He had no time to think about being winded as he was dragged at speed, rolled and tossed roughly in a purposeful direction. Between moments of catching his breath from the jolts and twists and turns as his body moved through leaves, he was bumped and scratched by debris on the ground. He tried to grab onto anything he could, yet branches whipped at his body – almost deliberately, he thought, *but how?*

The next moment he was rolling downwards into what appeared to be a deep pit. He felt a sense of relief; the rhythmical rolling was far more bearable than being dragged and scratched and bumped. Just as Jay hoped the ordeal would end, the energy that was moving his body ceased suddenly and he dropped the remaining short distance to the base of a pit, landing with a thud on a cold, oily, tarry-looking floor and immediately becoming aware of an extremely unpleasant smell around him. The smell was musty, reminiscent of rotten or decomposing things. He took a moment to inspect the areas of his body that hurt. His leg was considerably scratched and bleeding, but the adrenaline still racing through his body acted to block some of the discomfort. Jay took in the sights and smells around him and then heard snuffling. A concerning snuffling sound. There was a real heaviness to this breathing. What on earth would make such an unusual noise? Fear of the unknown took over, and Jay concluded that he was not in a safe place and his life was possibly in danger.

The snuffling and shuffling noises grew nearer and nearer. Jay could not see an immediate way out. The noise was not just coming from one thing, but several, and the only escape route was in the direction of the oncoming unknown, so was not an option. Jay realised he was in some sort of large cave or lair belonging to somebody or something. To avoid a confrontation with whatever was coming his way, he coiled into a submissive position and edged tight against the side of the pit. Clinging tight to his knees, he huddled up into a ball, hoping that whatever was about to arrive would take pity upon him.

He swallowed hard as he received the first glimpse of his unwelcome visitors. Coming out of the shadows, snuffling and shuffling, were the unsightliest creatures he had ever seen. They were short and stout, hog-like in appearance – black, oily animals. They were warty and drooled from the crevices at the corners of their jowly mouths. They walked on their hind legs in an almost human-like stance, but these creatures were far from human. Their razor-sharp teeth and deep-set, black-pupiled eyes with yellow whites made for a frightening sight. They seemed anxious with one another, grunting aggressively amongst themselves. They turned their attentions to Jay. One, possibly the leader of the grouping, jabbed at Jay with a trotter as if to check him over. Jay could not recall a time when he was so scared and worried. His heart raced and his legs trembled with fear, but he just allowed the scrutiny. Jubilation appeared to break out as the grunting reached a universal pitch coupled with the elevation of trotters as the hog-like creatures jumped up and down. Jay deduced from this commotion and their actions that he was of some delight to these beasts – friend as opposed to foe. His optimism soon receded as the creatures started to head back along the dark tunnel they had come from. Were they going to fetch someone or something else?

He adjusted his position, momentarily relieved that he had not been harmed. Perhaps his ordeal would now be over. Perhaps he could take this moment to escape. *Too late*. He heard more shuffling, different from the shuffling of the beastie hogs. There was a THUD between shuffles. The cave shuddered with every thudding footstep. Jay feared something huge, a beast of magnitude. A beast far worse than those he'd seen minutes before. He pushed his feet into the ground and tried hard to shuffle further back against the wall. Small pieces of grit dug into his hands as he did so.

A burst of fire shot through the opening, barely missing him. Jay jolted back, banging his head against the hard wall. He shivered with fright; trickles of sweat rolled down his forehead and his heart felt as if it would come through the cavity of his chest. The beast emerged into his focus. It was … it was … like a dragon! A mighty dragon-creature, like nothing he could ever have imagined. Storybooks had not done this creature justice. In the flesh it was astounding, horrific. It was all the things of nightmares, rolled into the form of a grotesque beast. As with the hog-like creatures, it too was dark and oily in appearance. It had the evilest of eyes and the eyes glared at him. Jay felt that the creature could read deep into his soul with its penetrating eyes. It could surely smell his fear as it leaned forward towards him. Its saliva stank the vilest of smells, drooling from its jowls just like the hog creatures' saliva did. As it did so, it dropped and coated Jay's head in sticky liquor. He felt physically sick but he dared not react. This was a creature that no being in their right mind would ever dare to challenge. The dragon-like creature snarled, revealing its razor-sharp teeth. There were traces of blood within its mouth. Jay wondered what it may have eaten recently; one snap from those jaws and his life would be ended.

He took some comfort from the fact that he had not been eaten up; his chances of survival were ever increasing. The longer he was spared from the jaws of this dragon-like creature the greater his chance of survival and possible escape would be. The hog-like creatures had returned in the background. They stood looking on making grunting noises. It was as if they were communicating with the dragon-creature, which appeared to respond. His voice was deep, gruff and loud, loud enough to make Jay want to cover his ears with his hands. Jay only presumed it was a 'he' as its voice was deep. The creature looked at Jay as if answering the hogs' questions. It then spoke – spoke in English, to Jay's complete surprise.

'He is from the human world.'

The hogs shuffled and stamped. Their energy heightened as more communication took place among the tribe.

'He is not the one, however. He is without wolvern.'

At this statement, the hogs settled back down, almost disappointed by the news. The dragon's voice had a sinister tone to it. Jay was trying to understand what world he was supposed to have come from and why he was not 'the one' and what a wolvern could be. He knew he must be of interest to the party, but he simply could not comprehend why.

'He must be stupid or perhaps very clever – the latter of the two I hope for his sake, at least. If he is not the one, then I suspect he came with the human one.' More grunting from the hogs, then a response. 'No … I'm not going to torture him.' The dragon stooped his head towards Jay. 'I've no need.' The dragon came closer and opened his hideous jaws. He breathed, then paused. 'Fetch me the traitorpathic ticks. The tick will do the torturing for me. Torturing of friendship and loyalty …'

With that, one of the hogs shuffled off at speed, returning moments later with a glass jar. Inside the dirt-stained jar were some spidery-looking creatures, equally as hideous as the hogs and evil dragon albeit far smaller. The traitor-pathic ticks scurried around frantically. The hog knocked the lid off the jar clumsily and swirled the jar around three times. The ticks stopped moving, seemingly stunned as if in some hypnotic state. The hog tipped one out onto the cave floor. The tick scurried around frantically until the dragon quickly caught hold of it in its firm lips with a delicacy Jay would not have expected from a beast of its size. He spat the tick directly onto Jay's arm. Within seconds Jay screamed out; his screams echoed through the cave as a burning sensation filled his arm. He could see the tick bur-rowing itself under his skin, leaving just the small hump of its back poking out of the surface. 'There,' said the dragon. 'That didn't hurt one bit … not for me anyway. Well, hu-man boy, with the traitorpathic tick in place, in a matter of seconds, you will have forgotten all about this episode. Your experience here today will be wiped clean from your memory. Get him back outside,' shouted the dragon in rage. There was a strong breeze, and the hogs cried out as if summoning something. From deep in the ground, shadows rose. The evil forms that had dragged Jay to the cave merged once again to create an energy force. They wrapped around him and bustled, tumbled and dragged him back the way he had come.

Chapter 7
Reunited

Having talked a while longer and answering more of Poppy's questions, Aviv and Ashen stated it was time for Poppy and Xania to leave and embark upon their journey. Aviv reminded Poppy of the changing moon and that time was of the essence. The elderly couple said they would walk with her to the border of Mayllis but would then leave Poppy to continue her travels, hopefully finding Jay along the way.

The sun was shining brightly and the sky was clear blue. The air was warm and momentarily Poppy lost all notion of the magnitude of the challenge she had to face. Ashen spoke about the lands of Nutash that included both Mayllis and Harifar, providing a brief account of each. Aviv, in passing, mentioned that Xania would be able to advise along the way. At this, Poppy looked at Aviv, confused as to how a wolf-bear animal would be able to advise her. She thought that either she must have misheard, or Aviv had meant to say something else. Before Poppy could question the remark, Aviv looked up towards the sky; she studied the moon and told Poppy that the New Blood Moon eclipse was not long away and that she and Ashen must leave her now. 'We are not protected beyond this border,' she said.

Poppy hugged the elderly couple and said that she would do what was required of her.

She was tempted, however, to just run back to the large dirt tunnel adjacent to the elderly couple's cottage. How easy would it be to just turn around and do that? She could slide back through the short tunnel and be once again back by the river. Her mother would be waiting, she could have tea, play with Dudley, everything would just be so simple again. Yet Poppy had found herself in a strange place and now felt committed to finding three dragonix eggshell pieces that would change the future of the land for the better. Why her? Why? There was also Jay. Jay was missing. Why did he have to go off? So frustrating. Everything was no longer straightforward, but a muddled mess. The thought of running back to the dirt hole could be an option if only she could find Jay. Where was he? He was her friend, her best friend, and she could not leave him. She needed to find him first. What if this were all just a dream, a strange and silly dream that she could just wake up from? Poppy thought that maybe if she gave herself a pinch she would wake up, but having pinched her arm, she still found herself walking the meadow in the sunshine with a large wolf-bear animal.

Poppy idly chatted away to Xania, not expecting a response, but this was all the company she had. As peculiar as it might seem though, Xania was good company. The wolf-bear had a gentle disposition, and this was reassuring. The pair walked side by side heading towards a hill. Poppy stopped just shy of the brow of the hill; she was positioned at the mouth of a huge valley of land. She could see for miles and the view was stunning, breathtaking. She paused for a moment, taking in the vast scenery. Looking at Xania, she asked, 'We haven't got to walk down there, have we?' With that, the animal turned its head and licked her hand and, in doing so, gazed almost reassuringly into her eyes. It appeared to communicate. 'Is that a yes?' Poppy said in a soppy high-pitched voice, surprised that the animal appeared to have responded with a lick. Although she realised not much could surprise her given her present situation – a strange land with strange people, and now she was walking with some strange animal. 'You are kidding me, aren't you?' was Poppy's next question. The animal looked once more but this time sneezed and shook its head. 'Right. That will be no then, I take it. And have we got to walk across that land to find what we're looking for?'

There was yet another confirming lick of the hand from Xania. Poppy felt at this point overwhelmed with uncertainty. Although this bear-wolf creature appeared to be giving her some answers, she just needed a hug, a hug from somebody to reassure her that everything would be alright. She needed something good to happen. Some help. Xania did not appear in the slightest bit aggressive, which was of some comfort. While ordinarily Poppy would not go towards any dog (or wild animal for that matter), Xania seemed to be of a calm temperament. She bent down on one knee, holding the strap of the animal's backpack, which Aviv had carefully attached when they were in the cottage, in one hand; she wrapped her other arm around the animal's neck. She nestled her face into the soft coat, feeling helpless as a tear trickled down her cheek. This bear-wolf creature would be the best substitute at this time for the hug she so desperately needed. Xania gave out a satisfying slow grumble, followed by a deep sigh. At that moment, Poppy felt comforted that everything would be fine. When she released herself from the hold, she couldn't help but laugh as the animal licked her face. She was reassured by the gesture, feeling that although Xania was an animal, she wasn't lonely after all. She had a friend who had her best interests at heart. 'Oh, you are so incredibly cuddly and cute!' She kissed the animal gently on the nose.

Not a moment later there was a sound. Poppy could hear something in the distance – the quickening of steps from behind. She turned. She could barely believe her eyes! It couldn't be, could it? It was Jay! Jay was running towards her from out of the dense forest in the distance behind. Poppy was filled with delight and relief, and a warm glow radiated through her body. She had so much to tell him. 'Jay! Jay! Xania look, it's Jay!' She ran towards him. 'Where on earth have you been?'

Jay quickened his steps, but it was clear from the way he was running that he was in some discomfort and was hurt. The distance between them closed. 'Jay. Where have you been? I've been so worried about you. I've so much to tell you. What's wrong with you? You're cut. You're bleeding.'

Jay caught his breath. 'Poppy. I don't know. I went over there.' He pointed towards the dense forest. Xania growled. 'I've bumped my head. I think I lost consciousness.' He paused and stared. 'What's that?'

'Jay, meet Xania. Xania is a wolvern.'

After the introductions, the three embarked upon their journey together, Poppy relayed the details of everything that had happened to her from the moment she first entered Nutash to all that Aviv and Ashen had told her – the prophecy, the dragonix Vasclaurus, and the three eggshells. Jay listened intently.

A couple of hours of walking and talking had passed. The heat was taking its toll on the three. Poppy suggested a short rest to take stock of their situation. There were some trees nearby bearing purple bulbous fruit. 'Xania, can we eat these?' she asked. Jay looked on with a worried expression, no doubt wondering why Poppy should be asking the advice of an animal. Xania once more licked Poppy's hand. 'I take that as a yes. Jay, it would appear we can tuck in. We also need to think about what we have learnt from forest school. Remember? Basic survival skills – we need food, water. We need to eat what we can and keep hydrated. We also need to set up a camp with a fire.'

'Agreed,' said Jay. He beckoned Poppy over to the trees. 'Get on my shoulders. You should be able to stretch up high enough to pick the fruit.' Following some giggling about the initial difficulty of getting onto Jay's shoulders, Poppy eventually managed to get balanced. She picked the fruit, dropping each one to the ground. 'If we pick more than we can eat, we can put the extra fruit into Xania's backpack. That way we'll have something for later. Yes, Jay?' Poppy encouraged Jay for an answer. 'You're not very talkative. What's the matter? Are you alright?'

'Yeah … I think so. My head just hurts a bit where somehow I took a blow to it.' Jay stooped down allowing Poppy to get off of his shoulders.

She opened Xania's backpack and placed the fruit in. 'Wow, Aviv thought of everything. There is some saphberry brew and some spare clothes by the look of things, although not quite my type of fashion!' Xania looked at Poppy and gave a slight grumble. 'I think that means we need to move on. Aviv told me there's one eggshell piece hidden somewhere in the land we are about to cross – Mayllis. Quite where, however, is anyone's guess! We need to actively search or ask but it will be like looking for a needle in a haystack and we haven't seen anybody to ask yet, so I am not sure how we'll find this eggshell.'

Xania wandered about during moments of pause as if keeping a check and lookout.

'Poppy, we need to stop and rest here. I'm not sure whether it's this bang to my head, but I feel really tired. I really don't think I can go any further.'

'Right. Are you completely sure? Although I guess it is getting dusky. Soon it will be nightfall and it will be difficult to see clearly where we're going. We can look to camp down for the night and set up a fire, but tomorrow we'll need to make up the time lost today. Agreed? We are against the clock, or rather moon I should say.'

'I know. Sorry. I just don't feel right.' Jay rubbed his brow.

Xania circled Jay, sniffing, then walked back and snarled.

'What's the matter with you? You silly dog ... wolf, bear, thing, whatever you are. It's Jay! What are you grumbling at him for?'

The three walked towards a circular patch of trees – a suitable area with shelter and a clearing for a campfire. As dusk fell, they set up camp. Poppy and Jay refuelled with fruit and saphberry brew. Xania appeared less settled and paced restlessly around the camp, eventually giving an almighty yelp. Poppy saw it was having difficulty walking. Xania lifted a front paw off the ground, placed it down and then picked it back up again as if weight-bearing were too uncomfortable. 'What have you done, you silly *dog*?' She walked over to the animal. 'Here, keep still and lift your paw. There had better not be any blood. I hate blood … which is odd because I want to be a vet when I grow up, so I might have to rethink that plan.'

She made Xania sit while she lifted the injured left front paw as gently as she could. 'Right – you have a very large thorn in the centre of your pad. That was silly, wasn't it! Keep still and I'll pull it out. Ready, on three. I'll be as quick as … I can't think of a simile so, well, anything that's quick! I could have said a cat I guess, but I would hate to offend you. Here we go, one … two … three!' Poppy gripped the thorn and pulled. 'There – out now. All better, hopefully. Oh, and there was blood, so thank you very much for that.'

Xania lay down and licked the small wound. Jay was fast asleep and had, it seemed, slept through the entire episode.

'We need to settle down now, Xania, and try to get a good rest.' Xania lay next to Poppy. Its thick fleecy coat made the animal the ideal camping companion, offering both warmth and comfort – a great combination. Poppy lifted her head and rested the nape of her neck in Xania's. She wrapped her arm as far across the animal's body as her own length would allow. Xania smelt of warm, clean fur – a comforting smell that soon had her drifting fast asleep.

Poppy awoke. She was aware that she had been asleep for some considerable time. She did not know what time it was – she imagined some time after midnight. It was dark, although the moon provided some welcome light. She awoke feeling cold and, turning over, realised Xania was missing. She was suddenly very alert. She sat up and immediately scanned the area. Having not managed to locate Xania, she rose to her feet to broaden her search. Poppy moved between tree and bush, whispering, 'Xania.' She could have simply shouted for the animal, but she didn't want to draw attention to herself; Aviv had warned her about certain aspects of Nutash.

She was beginning to think her search was in vain when she heard a twig snap behind her. She looked around. She stepped back, shocked, and her heart skipped a beat. She swallowed hard and took a deep breath in. There in front of her stood a boy. A boy! She grappled with her thoughts, wondering what on earth a boy would be doing in a wood in the middle of the night. Who was he? The boy was approximately her own age, but he was far more athletic in build than any of the boys in her year group. He was about Jay's height and his skin looked slightly tanned. His hair was ruffled and appeared a violet tone in the moonlight. She noticed the irises of his eyes; they were a stunning violet colour ... and they looked familiar. The two stared at each other, eyes locked in a fixed gaze. They remained like that for a moment. Although Poppy was stunned, there appeared nothing in the boy's character to suggest he was any threat to her. In fact, the opposite – he seemed strangely familiar, but how could that be? Poppy's mind raced as she started to make connections … she looked, she studied, the violet colouring … the eyes, the clothes similar to those she had seen in the backpack. She looked at the boy's left hand, which was wounded with a bloodstain in the centre. 'Xania … Xania … my gosh! Is … is that you?'

There was an unnerving pause, then, 'Yes …'

Chapter 8
The Land of Mayllis

'I don't understand,' said Poppy. 'What ... what are you? I thought ... I assumed you were a girl!'

'Sorry. I'm sorry you had to find out about me this way. It wasn't explained to you. Aviv and Ashen forgot to tell you. I know it's a shock and I'm sorry. I'm a wolvern. I can change state. Change into other things – just not things of flight. The dog, as you referred to me –' Xania seemed to find this amusing '– is my preferred state. I can achieve much of what I need to in that form and ... I guess it's appealing from a likeability point of view, would you agree? You seem to find me likeable in that form.'

Poppy did not know quite how to answer and felt somewhat embarrassed, so she did what she thought best – she deflected the embarrassment and covered up the comment with a sharp remark back. 'Well, actually … yes. I prefer the dog to the … boy thing you are now. It's cuter. But why *are* you a boy now? Why have you changed?'

'I need to communicate with you. You need to know where to go and where to search and who to ask to locate the dragonix eggshells. It's a little difficult to communicate by licking your hand or sneezing, would you not agree?' replied Xania.

'Oh, well, yes, there is that, I suppose,' said Poppy.

'I left it a while to share this secret because I wanted to build up a relationship, a bond with you first. Then I thought you'd trust me.' Poppy didn't quite know how to respond to that comment, so she said nothing. 'We will need to break this new information to your friend when he wakes.'

'Well … I don't know what Jay will think. He might feel he's severely concussed when he hears this news – it's just about enough for me to take in.'

'The sun is beginning to rise. We need to think about moving on. I will discuss with you and Jay what we need to do next.'

Poppy agreed with Xania's suggestion and the two walked back to where Jay was still peacefully sleeping.

Jay awoke and rubbed his eyes. He sat up slowly, peering around and taking in his surroundings. 'Wow! My head feels so much better now.'

'Well, that's as well. However, it may not do so after what I have to tell you. Are you sure you're alright and sitting comfortably?' Jay nodded, looking somewhat confused. 'You know Xania here? Yes?'

'Yes. I'm not confused Poppy, or stupid for that matter. I've just woken up. Give me at least one moment to compose myself.'

'Well, Xania is a wolvern who can change appearance – wolverns can change state.'

Xania walked from behind the tree and introduced himself. He sat down and explained everything to them. He talked all about his past, his family, and his magical abilities until he decided it was time to move on.

'We need to head to the heart of Mayllis – or rather where we will be likely to find somebody who knows something about the dragonix eggshells.'

The three collected up their belongings and set off on their travels.

'Hop on, conserve a little energy!' Xania metamorphosed back into his wolf-like preferred form. Poppy, with assistance from Jay, climbed onto his back.

The walk again was long but the glimpse of a town in the far distance kept their motivation going.

'When or if we find these eggshell pieces, how are we going to carry them?' Jay asked.

Poppy thought. 'I guess we can strap them to Xania's back. They must be robust if the pieces make up a dragonix's eggshell. We're not talking a delicate bird egg here, are we?'

'I guess not but dragons, or rather dragonixs are huge, aren't they? So how will a new one form in an eggshell so small and how does it reseal?'

'I asked Aviv and Ashen the same,' said Poppy. 'The eggshell pieces will just reseal with the magic of the New Blood Moon eclipse. The timing has to be just right. Then it will happen. The new dragonix forms and develops from foetus to baby to huge wonder instantaneously. As the egg hatches with its increasing size, the dragonix unfolds, expands and grows. The new dragonix is the oracle for the land, it looks after everyone and they all live happily ever after – you know the kind of thing. Unless of course disaster strikes as with this last egg hatching. Then it doesn't work out so well.'

'But what purpose does it serve?'

'Aren't you listening, Jay? I've just explained! It tends the land – governs the land. It's like … it's like … a prime minister.'

'A prime minister? Right … so there doesn't need to be a general election then or vote off because with each New

Blood Moon there's a change regardless. Wow! How simple is that?'

'Yes. Very. Now can we stop with the questions?'

Having paused for thought, Jay added, 'I think we could do with a dragonix back home ruling the country.'

Poppy looked at him with a raised eyebrow.

The town grew nearer and nearer and before the three could grow tired they reached the outskirts. Poppy slid off Xania's back while they walked down the steep hill into the town. The houses, shops, and taverns came in a variety of shapes and sizes and the stone exteriors were polygonal rubble, course square and Ashlar stone. They were not always perfect in stature; some chimneys were slightly crooked. The brickwork varied in colour – russet tones through to a range and variety of greys. The roads and side streets were paved with cobbled stone. There was noise and chatter and a liveliness to Mayllis ... or rather this small town within Mayllis. It appeared a busy, vibrant place in contrast to its rural surroundings.

As they walked into the town, the three received some inquisitive looks. 'I don't think they're dog friendly,' Poppy joked. Almost immediately Xania changed into human form and responded that he felt the interest was more to do with the 'human' visitors. The three continued to walk through the town ignoring the glances directed their way. Poppy wanted to blend in, although she couldn't help but notice the peculiar-looking people, and then there were the animals that behaved like humans. As Xania had said, it was she and Jay that looked out of place here.

'You looked lost!' The three turned around. The re-mark came from a fox-like animal with large endearing eyes – a little creature that fidgeted about. He beckoned them down a side street and in a squeaky voice said, 'I'm Alfski. Who are you looking for? Can I offer my humble services?'

'Can we trust him?' asked Poppy.

'Yes – he's trustworthy,' said Xania. 'We are looking for the three eggshell pieces to the dragonix's egg and we are in a hurry.'

Alfski shot backwards, apparently shocked by what he had just heard. He took stock and looked as if he were met-aphorically piecing eggshells together. He seemed to be searching for the answers to questions in his own mind.

After thinking for a while, he perked up and said, 'I can help you – quick.' He shot down another secluded alleyway, glancing left and right before he did so. He then beckoned the three again to follow him. 'We need to be discreet. You don't know who might be listening or watching. Your presence will not be welcome and if anyone gives Vasclaurus information, we could all be doomed! You will be the undoing of him, and of course the saving of Nutash. You are in danger. You need to see Grolban. Grolban will help you. He has been here since many New Blood Moons. He will know what you need to do. He will tell you. Come, follow me quickly.'

Vasclaurus squeezed himself through his cave and bellowed for his senior hog. 'Get me the traitorpathic ticks!' The hog shuffled at speed along a cave passageway and returned with a murky-looking jar. Four ticks scurried around inside. The hog clumsily fumbled with the jar lid. 'Hurry, you imbecile!' demanded Vasclaurus. The hog knocked the lid with its trotter and the lid toppled onto the stone floor. The hog then swirled the jar around three times to stun the ticks and then tipped one out onto the ground. It scurried around frantically. 'Quick!' Vasclaurus roared. The hog skirted around on its hind trotters following the tick then sucked it up into its mouth. 'I haven't got all day.' Vasclaurus's voice was now a little softer, although sinister in tone. 'Now, what do you taste? What telepathic messages are coming through?'

The hog pushed the tick around its mouth. Vasclaurus looked on as the hog's tongue licked continuously around its mouth. After a few seconds, the hog communicated to Vasclaurus what it knew. 'I see ...' said Vasclaurus. 'The time is growing nearer, and so are they, it would appear, nearer to causing problems. Hmm ... while I cannot alter the timing of the New Blood Moon, I can toy with these human young beings. The chosen one seems determined. How foolish of her. Time to put a few obstacles along the way, I think – that is what is required.' The senior hog nodded passionately in agreement. Vasclaurus moved his head from side to side slowly then elevated and depressed each shoulder as he stretched out his neck. His calm tone of voice and slow stretching movements were, he felt, the actions of a dragonix relaxed and very much in control. He noted, however, a glint of doubt in his chief hog's eyes as he dared to stare deep into his own. Did his chief hog detect the tiniest glimmer of fear? How dare he show doubt. Infuriated by what he had perceived, Vasclaurus bellowed and sent him on his way.

Alfski led the three to an antique shop. Through the large bay window, Poppy could see it was filled with clocks and chimes and unusual timepieces – a cavern full of trinkets and delights in gleaming metals, some with decorative gems. A large ox-like creature guarded the door. 'We need to see Grolban,' Alfski said.

'You cannot enter without a groober,' was the reply from the shop bodyguard.

'Well, we haven't got a groo—' With that, Xania slunk behind the others and metamorphosed into a groober. 'There,' Alfski replied, somewhat surprised having looked around. 'We are with groober. Now we need to enter, for time is of the essence.' The shop bodyguard moved aside and gestured to the back of the shop. The four followed in the direction given.

They wandered towards the back and down a winding wrought-iron staircase. They were met with a dusty workshop and shelves upon shelves that held broken trinkets and timepieces. So many soon-to-be-mended wonderful things. They heard a gruff cough coming from the far back. They paused.

'Who is it and what do you want?' said a stern voice.

The visitors moved towards the back of the workshop to where the voice was coming from. Xania, having been acknowledged in groober form, swiftly metamorphosed to human form and explained the reason for their visit. 'We've come to find the dragonix eggshell pieces. We need your help.'

There was a momentary pause.

'You've come about the dragonix eggshell pieces? Well, well. Come forward and let me view you. Your arrival has been long awaited. I never thought I would live long enough to see this day, and yet here it is.' Grolban was a stout troll-like individual. His face was not unpleasant. He had a bushy grey beard and old-looking eyes. The pupils of his eyes were opaque. Poppy wondered if the strain of focusing on fixing intricate objects must have taken its toll on the dear old troll over time. He didn't look directly into her eyes; she thought he probably struggled to see clearly. It dawned on her just how important the eyes were in bringing about a sense of emotional connection. His fingers were grubby, no doubt from working with old, dusty trinkets. He had little silver highly magnified spectacles that balanced on the end of his round stubby nose. He tilted his head down to get a better view through his spectacles.

'Do you know about the eggshell pieces – where they are?' asked Xania.

'Where they are?' Grolban studied Xania.

'Yes, we need to find them quickly.'

'Well, you've come to the right place. I do know. I do indeed. Or at least the whereabouts of two of them. So you are in luck. One I have in my possession. A raspin, who was a dear friend of my departed sister, gave it to my sister for protection, fearful that it would be found by one of Vasclaurus's evil subjects. They searched far and wide for it. Still do for that matter. When my sister departed from this world, her last request was that I keep it safe for when the time came. The time that a human child would need it as the prophecy foretold. And here you are. So, I have one piece. The other is kept somewhere in the land of Harifar. The third, I am afraid, was taken during the eclipse and its whereabouts ... well ... is unknown. I am sorry I cannot give you that information. But all is not lost. There is always hope. Hope and determination may well see you through your quest along with a little help. You might already be aware that after today, you have only two days until the eclipse of the New Blood Moon. So, time is running out indeed. I can give you the first piece. If you make haste, you can reach Harifar by dawn tomorrow on foot. As soon as you reach there, you will need to call the flutterbugles as soon as you cross the border. They, I understand, have kept the secret of the second eggshell piece well. Now, there is no time to lose. Come hither.'

They followed Grolban back up the iron staircase and into the shop. 'Now, the first eggshell piece you seek, I have kept in the green-fronted shop at the end of the street. I will meet you there just as soon as I have got myself together and closed this shop. You are quicker on foot than I. Go in and down the steps towards the back as you did here. You will find a chest. The key to the chest is hidden under the sixth floorboard from the back. Tell Nelda, as you approach, that you are my special guests. She will know. She is very sweet. Now – on your way.' As they were about to leave the shop, Grolban handed Poppy a timepiece. 'There,' he said. 'This is very special. You have no need to worry. You will know when to use it. It will tell you when the time comes, but you will only have five minutes of time, so conserve it well. This, young man,' he said to Jay, 'is a whistlewinder. You will need it to summon the flutterbugles. You take charge of it. Now off you go and I will follow shortly.'

Grolban stumbled on his doorstep. Xania and Alfski helped him, indicating Jay and Poppy should run ahead. Poppy approached the green-fronted shop. Jay was transfixed by the shop next door. 'Come on, Jay, we need to go in.' Jay stopped and scratched the top of his arm. 'What are you doing Jay? Come on!'

'We need to go in here, Poppy.'

'No, we don't. It's the green-fronted shop. Remember? Hurry. We've no time to lose.'

'Look,' said Jay. 'The décor's green inside. You're wrong, Poppy. Look – this is the shop. You've got the wrong one.' Poppy switched direction and peered inside the window. The shop appeared to be an unusual pet shop. It was filled with cages, homes to the sweetest and cutest-looking peculiar baby animals. 'Ah! They're so cute!'

'I know – and there's the lady. Look, she's smiling. Grolban did say sweet, didn't he? You must have misheard him, Poppy – it's a green shop inside. Come on, let's go in.'

Poppy opened the door and she and Jay entered.

'Hello, we are guests of Grolban,' Poppy announced. The woman smiled and Poppy couldn't resist bending down to take a closer look at a stunningly colourful and beautiful furry ball of fluff staring at her from a cage. It had large ears that flopped over its huge round bright glistening eyes. Before Poppy could ask, the woman had unlocked the cage and had the curious creature in her arms. Poppy gently took hold of it; she stroked it and was completely mesmerised.

She stood up and saw Xania, Grolban and Alfski at the door. Xania had a look of horror on his face. His eyes widened and eyebrows furrowed. He was clearly trying to open the door, but it appeared to be locked … he was doing his best to turn the handle, yet the door would still not open. She sensed his urgency and walked towards the door as Xania, Alfski and Grolban pushed it with all their might to no avail. Poppy felt a sharp sustained pinch in her hand. The creature had bitten down hard, sinking its teeth into her flesh. She felt a burning sensation deep inside her arm.

She squeezed her wrist to try to dispel the pain, but the burning sensation continued to creep further up her arm … she was helpless to stop it. It spread across her chest. Her chest muscles tightened and her breathing shallowed. It was as if someone were squeezing around her neck. The room began to swirl around. She gasped for breath and was overcome with dizziness; she felt her legs wobble … then … nothing.

Xania saw Poppy fall as he looked through the windowpane in the door. His stomach was ablaze with a fireball of anger. There was no time to lose. Taking the form of a wolvern, he scuttled back to get a good run-up before pounding the door through with his sheer power and strength. His heart thudded with the surge of adrenaline running through his body. He leapt forward, landing right next to Poppy, lowered his head and sniffed her. His nose touched her cheek; she felt cold and her skin looked grey. The shop was also turning grey. The change in colour crept eerily down from the ceiling to the walls to the floor. The animals within the shop turned ashen grey, then to stone, then crumbled to dust. With that, so did the rest of the shop – the walls, the ceiling, the counter and the shopkeeper all crumbled to dust. All that was left was Poppy, on the floor and motionless, with Jay, Grolban and Alfski looking on helplessly.

Grolban moved forward. 'This is the work of some very bad magic. I know not how but someone knows you are here, and I already have my thoughts as to who. Look at her hand – teeth marks and blood – she's been bitten. Do something quick … you can help her.' Xania gnawed at Poppy's wound, licking frantically to draw out the poison. He periodically shook his head as he spat out the poison. 'Keep going,' Grolban encouraged. 'It's working. It is working. Her colour is returning.'

Poppy started to stir. Her eyelids flickered, she gasped for air and then opened her eyes. She took a minute to come to and sat up slowly. 'What … what happened?' she asked.

Xania returned to his more human form. 'You were bitten. Bitten by a creature with a deadly poison. It was a trap. Whatever made you come in here?'

'I thought … I thought this was the shop,' Jay said.

'You thought! You could have killed her – got yourselves killed for that matter. What were you thinking of? Whatever possessed you to do such a thing? Why would you want to deviate and go inside a pet shop? Why?' Xania demanded an answer for what appeared to be utter stupidity. He paced around then having calmed himself continued. 'We have so little time left.'

'Are you feeling well enough to continue Poppy?' Xania asked. 'I can carry you if you are weakened from this dreadful ordeal.' He shot Jay a look. Having conveyed his disdain with a stare, he changed back to a wolvern and helped Poppy onto his back.

'Here, take my old walking stick too. It might be of some help,' insisted Grolban.

'Thank you,' said Poppy as she took hold of the walking stick.

'Now let's get inside,' said Grolban.

Poppy finally entered the intended shop with Xania, Jay, Grolban and Alfski. She and the others greeted Nelda briefly and then without delay headed down the staircase to the room below. Just as Grolban had told them, she saw it: the chest. Alfski scurried ahead to the back and counted in six floorboards. He glanced back at the others; Grolban looked around the space, fixed his eyes on something then raised his index finger in the air as if to suggest he was about to say or do something. He walked over to a shelf as quickly as his ageing joints would allow him and handed Alfski a lever, which Alfski inserted just under the floorboard. Poppy felt a little redundant, but her friends seemed to have the situation in hand so she thought it best not to interfere. Alfski jumped up and down and the floorboard lifted. A trickle of excitement buzzed around inside her. Grolban helped to prise the floorboard up further. Poppy moved across to look underneath. There, directly below, was a delicately detailed bronze key. Alfski grabbed it and scurried to the chest without delay. He placed the key inside the lock and turned it carefully anticlockwise. The lock clicked. Grolban and Alfski stood at each end, nodded to each other and then strained to lift the lid. It must have been stiff or of some considerable weight. Inside, covered over with a woven blanket, was the eggshell piece in all its glory. Poppy stared. No one spoke. She thought, like her, they were taking a moment to digest what they saw. The eggshell piece was extraordinary – nothing like she had imagined it would be. It was beautiful. Iridescent. It glowed in the dim light of the shop. It was no ordinary eggshell; it was truly magnificent.

Poppy was the first to break the silence. 'I never knew a piece of eggshell could be so beautiful.' It dawned on her in that moment of awe and wonder that here was something magical. The stuff that fairy tales were made of. This was real, and she had a purposeful job to do. Such a beautiful fragment deserved to be put together, resealed with its two other pieces. Made entire and whole. And there was the matter of the new dragonix that would be born from the egg. What would that look like coming from such a stunningly beautiful egg? The land of Nutash would be restored to its former glory just by the resealing of the pieces.

Poppy felt a surge of motivational energy rising within her. She looked at the others. They were all glowing with excitable vigour. They were now truly on a mission – a mission to save Nutash.

Chapter 9
The Land of Harifar

Poppy held on tight to Xania as they left Mayllis for Harifar. She felt the gentle motion of his stride both soothing and relaxing, and as the movement rocked her gently to and fro she felt sleepy. Just for a short time she was at peace and decluttered of her anxieties from her recent frightening experience.

Little was said on the journey. Alfski hopped and skipped along the way with an abundance of energy and enthusiasm topped with a sprinkling of innocence. He was quite a gregarious little character. Poppy took a stronger grip of Xania's soft fur and considered what a wonderful animal he was. She had grown fond of him. She liked him in this form because he reminded her, in essence, of Dudley, her pet dog. Dudley was attentive, gentle, kind and affectionate. Dudley was often there for her to stroke or cuddle in times of calm or sadness. Some breeds of dogs were said to be intelligent. Poppy was not convinced that Dudley was particularly intelligent, but he did have a bond with her, there was a sharing of equal fondness. This was how she perceived her relationship with Xania. Xania had her best interests at heart and she almost felt a void when she thought about what would become of them when this journey ended ... how would she feel about leaving Xania? 'Parting is such sweet sorrow,' came to mind. Poppy thought that Shakespeare must have experienced a meaningful relationship, just like she had, to inject such compassion between the characters Romeo and Juliet. She wrapped herself around Xania tightly, taking care not to crush the bag containing the precious eggshell piece. She drifted and stirred gently between pockets of semi-consciousness.

Xania was lying down. Poppy must have fallen asleep and only woke to hear him say that dawn had broken and they must move on. Harifar was within reach. They walked through a field knee-high in rushes, the stems of which supported colourful bell-headed blossoms that swayed and sweetly rang, which Poppy and Jay found delightful.

'We are here. This is Harifar. There is the start of the enchanted forest,' Xania informed them.

'Is there a town?' asked Jay.

'No,' said Xania. 'It's all fields and there is a forest and river area, all surrounded by these melobell stems. It's home to flutterbugels and other creatures.'

'Why do we have to go through the forest? Can't we just go around? It looks far more pleasant and surely the terrain will be easier to navigate?' asked Poppy.

'It will take too long. This is the narrowest area. We do not have the time to deviate, I am afraid. We need to head straight on. Jay, you will need to wake the flutterbugels with your whistlewinder now.'

'Where are they?' Jay asked.

'They are asleep within the melobells. Their peaceful dreaming is the gentle melody you heard when walking through the stems.'

Jay removed the golden whistlewinder from his back pocket. He inspected it momentarily, lightly polishing the metal with his T-shirt. He took the mouthpiece to his lips and blew gently. The noise that radiated from the instrument had a high but delicate pitch that seemed to fill the void stretching far and wide. The subtle swaying from the melobells increased steadily, and hundreds upon hundreds of colourful fairy-like creatures fluttered around for a few moments then flew towards one another. What were many individual flutterbugels soon became one uniform cloud floating in the air, lightly tossed to and fro by the wind. Xania called out and upwards, as if talking to the sky, that they were looking for the dragonix eggshell piece. There was a momentary swaying and shifting from the flutterbugels as they took note of the question and then the answer came forth in a harmonic chorus: 'It is hidden in the wishing well beyond the river.'

'Come on, we must follow them – they will take us towards the place,' said Xania. 'There is no time to lose.' The flutterbugels dispersed; some went back to sleep in their bell blossoms, while a large handful guided the way. An occasional curious one would take a moment to stop and investigate its special visitors and perch on either a nose or a shoulder.

They entered the forest area. Poppy was immediately aware that it was not dissimilar to a rainforest. The trees were very tall. The place had a clear forest floor, understorey, canopy and emergent layer. The flutterbugels flew ahead, turning and hovering every so often to encourage Xania, Poppy and Jay to follow. Alfski, being nimble and quick, was able to move at pace. The forest was humid but it was not quiet. There were strange noises that could have been coming from the chirping birds. There were other sounds that may have belonged to other equally strange creatures that only one could imagine in their mind's eye. On occasions Poppy would catch the odd glimpse of something quite marvellous and interesting in appearance.

They came to a large pool of relatively clear water. Poppy could see a variety of fish and amphibian-type animals moving around beneath the surface. Every so often, something came up as if to inspect the unusual visitors before going on its way again. There were colourful lily-type pads that adorned the water with their beauty. Xania, Poppy, Jay and Alfski paused to assess how best to cross the water.

Poppy's interest was piqued as Alfski identified large raised stones in the water and used them as his pathway across. He then found a log that bridged the bigger distance between the final two stones. 'We could swim, but I guess trying to get across as Alfski has will be quicker,' she said. Xania went first in wolvern form, looking towards Poppy and encouraging her to follow. The stones were a little slippery and they had to take care. Travelling dry, Poppy thought, would be far more comfortable than being in soaking wet clothing from swimming as she had previously suggested.

She began to feel uncomfortable. Not physically, but she sensed a change in the ambient surroundings. The noises appeared to diminish. The sun peeping through the canopy layer dimmed. The sky became a black mist of crawling doom. Poppy was certain she saw something dark, of considerable size, way in the distance of her peripheral vision. The once clear water went murky and the warm air cooled.

'We are in danger,' the flutterbugels chorused. At that moment, there was some agitation in the water. A large fish leapt up from out of the blue. It flew towards Poppy and its huge lips covered her face. The force of the fish knocked her off the stone and it pushed her deep down into the water. Poppy struggled to hold her breath and fought with all her might. As she wriggled, the desire to breathe overcame her. She knew she couldn't draw breath because she would drown. She frantically pulled at the fish, but the suction was too strong. She didn't know how much longer she could hold her breath and inside she was crying. Despite the feeling of impending doom, Poppy became aware of something sizable splashing into the water, and hoped against hope it was someone come to rescue her.

It felt as if something was tugging the fish from her face. There was some sort of struggle and resistance to the tugging, and all at once the fish was no longer attached. She kicked to the surface. Gasping for breath, but relieved, she swam towards one of the large stones and, placing her weight on her forearms, began to pull her body up and out of the water. Alfski and Jay threw a vine towards her. She clutched hold of it with her left hand. Xania raced across the stones towards her. Poppy knew she was now in safe hands. Xania would help her and pull her out from the water; she was so exhausted. As she knelt on one knee about to stand up another fish leapt out of the water and flew towards her. She managed to take a breath before her face was covered again by another huge sucker fish. Before she knew it, she had been forced back deep under the water.

Poppy felt another disturbance in the water. As she struggled for breath, thrashing her arms, her right hand felt fur. *Xania*, she thought. Again she felt as if the fish were being tugged off her face, then relief once more as she was free to kick up to the surface. She attempted to pull herself up onto the stone, coughing and spluttering and shielding her face in her folded arms every time she caught a glimpse of fish leaping back and forth, petrified she'd be dragged under again.

She was distraught and did not know how much more of this ordeal she could take. Tears rolled down her face – there seemed no escape from death. She couldn't have held her breath any longer when she was under, and it was a miracle that she managed to resurface in time. All thanks to Xania. She peered up as she felt something touch her arm. It was another vine, thrown to her by Alfski. She grabbed it but knew she would never get out of the pond safely in the face of the continued onslaught. She became aware of a throbbing warmth coming from her back pocket. Lying across the stone, still holding the vine, she reached back with her free hand and fumbled to reach the source of the heat. It was the timepiece Grolban had given her. She pulled out the object. The hands on the face of the clock shone and glowed brightly. Still gasping for breath and turning her face away sharply from the fish as they continued to fly at her, she intuitively pressed the button on the timepiece. With that very action, everything completely stopped. The darting fish froze in time, totally motionless. All was still, except Xania, Jay, Alfski and herself. Poppy was aware of her heavy breathing in the midst of the silence, and she took the time to inhale deeply. She could hear her heart beating, pounding within the cavity of her chest. As she focused and slowed each inhalation, she felt her heartbeat beginning to fall back to its normal rhythm. Exhausted, she slowly climbed out. She walked steadily across the stones supported by Xania. 'Are you hurt?' he asked.

'No. Just my pride.' With her hands on her knees and bent over she regained her composure and glanced in Jay's direction. He was scratching his arm again. 'Jay, how come you're managing to get away with not being eaten by crazy flying fish? Or bitten by cute creatures?'

'I don't know. I feel really bad for you. I wish it was me instead of you.'

'I would imagine, as Poppy is the protected one of the two of you, she is the one that could cause the greatest amount of harm for those of the Dark Side. She could be the cause of their demise and destruction through the re-sealing of the three eggshells. She is, therefore, clearly the target here – someone wants her killed,' Alfski said.

'We must move on,' urged Xania. 'That is as long as you are able to, Poppy.'

Poppy nodded to indicate that she was ready to continue with the journey.

'The timepiece! Poppy, you need to restart time now you're out of danger. Remember, Grolban explained – you only have five minutes,' said Jay. It was helpful that Jay had given her that reminder, but Poppy wondered why he couldn't have been more helpful earlier when she really needed him. He had stood back and done absolutely nothing.

Poppy pressed the button and the rainforest returned to its former glory, as it had been minutes before the dark magic fell upon it.

'Well … I only have two minutes of time left. That's not much. I hope I won't need to use more than that again.'

Poppy looked towards Jay and couldn't help thinking about his actions. As they all walked on, Jay continued to scratch his arm. 'Why do you keep scratching your arm?' she asked.

'I don't know. I think I've been bitten. It itches and stings.'

'Let me see.' She looked closely. 'I think it's a bite and you're having a reaction to it. There appears to be a dark spot. You've made it bleed.' Poppy gave Jay a hug, and he hugged her back. He was a good friend and Poppy didn't like to think that he was not happy or hurt in any way. Any doubtful feelings she'd had about him earlier started to disappear.

The four continued. Alfski spotted the well first. They approached the crumbling font and Jay peered in. He immediately stepped back when a troll-like creature poked his head out irritably. He was covered in moss and it was not clear where his skin started and the moss ended. 'We have come for the eggshell,' said Poppy. 'The flutterbugels have directed us here.' The troll was not forthcoming with his response and appeared to do all he could not to cooperate. His lack of urgency was frustrating for them all. Poppy stressed the importance of having the eggshell piece. The troll finally invited her to fetch it out from deep within the well. Poppy thought the troll was probably lonely and had previously withheld the information about the eggshell piece in order to keep his unexpected guests, who offered company, there longer. She went to pull up the large bucket in the hope the eggshell would be within it, but the chain that should have been connected to the bucket was detached.

'How are we going to get it?' she asked. 'Think – we need to think quickly!' Poppy looked up to the sky in panic. Xania did the same. She could see the sun and moon drawing closer together now.

'The flutterbugels. They could help. The whistlewinder,' Alfski said. Jay took out his whistlewinder and blew it softly. Within seconds there was a flurry of the delicate little creatures once more. Poppy and Jay explained what needed to be done. The flutterbugels made a long chain by linking themselves to each other and fluttered down into the well. Moments later, they returned.

In unison, they spoke. 'It is not there.'

'It must be!' cried Poppy. 'Where is it?' She turned her attention to the troll.

'It's not here,' he said.

'Well, where is it?' said Poppy, growing impatient. 'You know we have to find the other piece before the eclipse of the New Blood Moon!'

The troll seemed unperturbed. 'I cannot tell you … but then I can,' he reflected.

'What does that mean?' Poppy said, incredibly frustrated by now.

Xania walked closer. 'He's a riddle troll,' he said. 'This is not the ideal situation for us at this stage in our journey.'

'So, what does that mean?' Poppy was filled with despair. 'Can you just tell us?' she pleaded.

'I can,' said the troll. 'Look for the red-spotted amphibian. It is buried next to where it … is sitting!'

'Oh gosh!' Poppy said. 'I'm *not* going back to that pond. Please! This is not a game.'

Time was wasted pacing around, with frustrations continually raised to the troll, but it was all in vain. Jay said he would walk to the pond and look. The others searched the area around the well. The sun and moon continued to creep closer and closer together.

Then Poppy spotted the subject of the riddle. She ran. 'It's here! The red-spotted amphibian. I've worked out what it is. It is a toadstool!' She fell to her knees and began to scuff the soil away with her hands. 'Help me!'

Xania ran over and by her side pawed swiftly but gently, brushing the dirt away. There, underneath hands and paws, light shone through the soil … a gleaming familiar sight they recognised, a sparkling iridescent glazed exterior. It was here. Hidden deep within the ground was the second piece. The jagged edges looked like they would slot perfectly together with those of the first.

'Great. We need to move on,' said Xania looking up at the sky. The sky was darkening, the sun not so bright. It was as if it were expecting change to come. The moon had an unusual haze around it and the blue sky it hung in was now streaked pink and green. It looked beautiful as dusk fell, although its message was far from beautiful. 'Tomorrow is the last day. The eclipse will happen then. Time is running out and we have one last piece to find.'

'What are we going to do?' said Poppy. 'We have no idea as to its whereabouts – we could be searching anywhere. We have no clues this time.'

'Well … you might be needing another riddle to know who has the other piece and where it might be,' said the troll, who had clearly been listening to them. 'But I might want something in return.' He looked at the shiny whistlewinder Jay was holding.

'We don't have time for games! Is this what you want? Jay, give it to him. Here – you can have it, but we need a clue,' said Poppy.

The troll wrote in the sand. 'I cross, so be "ongard" blue and green that's the sign once you've seen.' He finished by saying, 'That is all I can tell you.'

The four, although confused initially at this riddle, accepted that they were not going to receive any more information, and they had no time to plead with the troll to provide more clues. The likelihood was that the answer, if they could guess it, would lead them to the final eggshell. Poppy etched the riddle within her memory.

'Right. We must not delay. For the time being, let's just head towards the Rocky Peak,' said Xania. 'The nesting place is there on the brow of the mountain. That is where you must reseal the three eggshell pieces during the eclipse. It makes perfect sense for you to be there regardless, Poppy. The Rocky Peak is your end point. We will go now and think about the riddle on route. If we can solve it between now and then, saving Nutash could be well within our sights. We may need a little extra help though. Flutter-bugels, I need you to listen to my plan.'

Chapter 10
The Darker Side

Aviv and Ashen were surprised and thrilled to see a handful of flutterbugels. They delighted in hearing the recent news. To learn that Poppy had two eggshell pieces already and the saving of Nutash was within her grasp filled them with immense joy. They knew that Vasclaurus being defeated and Nutash being restored was now truly a reality if only the final eggshell piece could be found. Excitement grew within them as they listened to the flutterbugels. They heard how a crowd was gathering in Mayliss and that Grolban was taking charge of a newly recruited army of keen supporters. 'We are going to fight for Nutash – we are going to support the human one to accomplish this quest! We are going to unite and conquer our fears so that we can return our land to its former glory, no matter what. We are going to reclaim Nutash!' he had said. They were treated to an account of the deafening roar of rapturous applause that followed from the crowd, and were told how the cheers and shouts could be heard all over the land. They were informed of how the empowered crowd raced to collect various items and tools, and anything that could be used as weapons if so required.

Aviv and Ashen were filled with hope. The resealing of the shell and birth of a new dragonix could take place as the prophecy stated, just in the nick of time. They bade their farewells as the flutterbugels flew off in haste, heading in the direction of Mayllis.

Aviv and Ashen, although elderly, and not protected across the border, decided that if Nutash were to be saved, it would require everyone to help, no matter what the consequences. If Poppy could demonstrate the level of bravery she had at such a tender age, with her whole life ahead of her, they could join the army and put their lives on the line to assist. They decided that they would travel to Mayllis also. 'Once we reach Mayllis, we can gain transportation to Harifar,' Ashen said. 'Hurry, dear.'

As they were about to leave there was a knock on their door. The couple were confused as to who would be calling on them. Ashen went to the keyhole and peered through, to find a somewhat older but familiar face on the other side.

He stepped back, surprised. He turned to look at Aviv.

'Who is it, dear? You looked shocked.'

'You'll never guess … I-I can't believe it!'

Xania, Poppy, Jay and Alfski walked on, desperately trying to solve the riddle. Poppy and Jay were attempting to make associations with things that might be blue or green when Jay had an enlightenment: 'Sometimes riddles are anagrams!'

Poppy agreed and searched her mind frantically to make connections. 'Hold on!' She dropped to her knees and knelt down in a sandy patch of soil. She scribed some letters in a different order over and over again with her forefinger. She swiped the sand with each new attempt. 'That's it!

That's it!' she cried, spelling it out in the sand. 'It is an ana-gram. I thought there was a spelling mistake. Ongard, without the letter *u* you would expect in the word *guard*, contains the letters for dragon! The troll also said, "I cross". So, if you look at *cross* as a symbol, or rather a letter, and *I* as the letter I, put them together – you've got the word drag-onix!'

'Right … it would appear that that is where we're head-ing,' said Xania. 'Vasclaurus must have the final piece. So now we know, but this is not as we hoped – this is not going to be easy, he's not going to give it up without a good fight. We will have some battle to get it.'

There was a moment of silence while the four consid-ered the situation.

Xania seemed particularly deep in thought as if he knew what was coming. 'We cannot do this alone,' he said. 'While the flutterbugels have gone to Mayllis to find help, this won't be enough – we will need the help of everyone and everything that will offer their life.'

Poppy stepped back. The land for as far as she could see spun around. She assumed she would just need to reseal three eggshell pieces. The thought of a battle, fighting, was not something she had considered. She was overcome with fear. Her stomach filled with butterflies and her heart raced. A flush of adrenaline filled her and the palms of her hands felt sweaty. She swallowed hard and then composed herself. She knew the time was drawing near and there was no turning back. Nutash was relying on her. She could not let all its inhabitants down.

Xania let up a howl so loud and mighty it filled the land. Within minutes, creatures of all shapes and sizes and looks appeared on the distant hills; trees came to life, and their roots took the form of legs and branches like arms as they strode across the land; patches of grass were overturned to soil as creatures crawled from out of the earth; so many creatures flocked from the woods and sky. Here was an army – an army that was going to find the final eggshell piece and fight anything that stood in their way.

The previously quiet area of the land was now filled with activity as the army continued to build. In the distance were hundreds more creatures, some riding on the back of animals. Xania changed to human form.

'These are friends, aren't they?' Poppy asked.

'Yes,' said Xania. 'They are from Harifar and beyond, looking at the numbers. All is good.'

Once all the creatures had assembled Xania gathered the army. He climbed up onto a pile of rocks to deliver his plan. They would need to enter the Dark Side and track Vasclaurus down. Xania predicted Vasclaurus's army would come forth immediately to protect their leader. 'Each should be terminated with a direct hit to their core. This is their weak area – it is the depth of their dark soul which will cause disintegration to the rest of their body … they will then turn to dust. A careful eye must be kept for the third eggshell piece.' Xania identified a group to focus purely on the tracking down of the eggshell. 'If you come across Vasclaurus, remember he is mighty and dangerous. He has three skills in his favour. Flight, fire and size. If you have a clear target, aim for his eyes. If he has no sight his ability is weakened, although he will not be destroyed. Poppy, you will remain with me. Once the eggshell has been found, it will be brought to the Rocky Peak. We will head there together. I cannot protect you in the Dark Side, so we will be best not entering it. Jay, you will join us.'

Xania metamorphosed back to wolvern form. He moved slowly through the sea of bodies to sip water from the stream. The crowd parted in respect.

Poppy looked through the army of creatures. Her heart fluttered when she saw Aviv and Ashen. Delighted to see friendly faces, she waved. As Aviv waved back, Poppy's moment of delight was interrupted as Jay pulled her arm sharply. 'Look, Poppy, look! In the woods, a bluey-green light. It's flickering. Poppy, come on!'

'We can't,' Poppy said. 'We need to wait. Aviv and Ashen are here. We need to wait for Xania's instruction. I'll call for him.'

'No!' Jay shouted. 'We don't have time. We need to do this. Xania will follow. That light might be something alerting us to the eggshell. Come on!' Jay ran towards it. Poppy had lost Jay once before and she was not going to run the risk of doing so again. She ran, but shouted back to Xania. She raced after Jay to the border of the forest.

Xania turned ... he was momentarily shocked as he couldn't believe what he was seeing. He wanted to warn Poppy and Jay but it was too late. He watched helplessly as he saw them being drawn into the Dark Side's invisible barrier. Xania was distracted from his thoughts for a moment as Alfski leapt onto his back, then he considered the flashbacks in his mind – flashbacks of Jay's scratching, Jay being drawn into the wrong places, encouraging Poppy to go along with him, not helping at the pond, his disappearance early on, the bite. Xania metamorphosed to human form mid-run; having pieced together the clues he turned his head round and shouted to Alfski, 'He's leading Poppy into a trap! He's infected! He's been infected with a traitor-pathic tick. We've been tracked all along. You need to get to him and get that traitorpathic tick out!' Xania metamorphosed back to a wolvern and continued his run at a great pace, only to stop dead as the barrier refused him entry. He could not protect Poppy on the Dark Side. He had known this would be the case, but it had been worth trying. He watched Alfski leap through.

Poppy heard a rustling of leaves and saw Alfski scurrying towards her. He looked extremely worried. He said nothing to her but immediately jumped onto Jay's shoulder. Poppy looked on in shock as she saw Alfski digging his claw deep into Jay's arm. 'What are you doing to him?' Jay shouted out as the claw dug in; blood trickled down his arm. Gnawing quickly, Alfski drew out a black creature with a lot of legs. In no time at all he had dropped it on the ground and was pulling it apart with his claws. It put up a good fight; even with half its body dismembered, its legs continued to move. Eventually it stopped and gave up life. Poppy looked on, completely flabbergasted, Jay transfixed and horrified. 'What on earth is it?' he said.

'It's a traitorpathic tick,' Alfski said. Alfski briefly explained that Jay must have been infected with it at some point when he was alone. Poppy pieced together clues from the time that Jay had gone missing when he first entered Nutash. Jay went very quiet; he rubbed his head, his eyes dazed. Poppy could almost see him piecing events together. His eyes welled up with tears, and Poppy watched as one teardrop trickled slowly from one of his eyes.

'I'm so sorry, Poppy.' Jay looked completely mortified. He must have felt riddled with guilt. Poppy knew Jay would never want to hurt her. Her eyes filled with tears, knowing Jay would be heartbroken. She threw her arms around him and assured him that none of this was his fault – he was purely the innocent victim of an evil plan over which he had no control.

The reassurances were soon interrupted by a rumbling and trembling of the ground. 'What is that?' Poppy said.

The Nutash army had now entered the forest. There was noise and commotion as they filled the space – so many bodies and creatures heading in different directions at pace on a mission to search for the final eggshell piece. Poppy could see Aviv and Ashen in the distance but she became distracted as a strong breeze seemed to form around her; leaves started to swirl. An eerie energy built as the ground erupted with ghostly dark figures; grotesque hogs and beasts drooling and growling and moaning seemed to appear from nowhere. Poppy felt Jay grab her arm. 'I've dreamed this once before,' he said. He stepped slightly in front of her as if to protect her. The creatures increased in number and were now swamping the Nutash army. Poppy looked on utterly shell-shocked as some of the Nutash creatures and people were unlucky and fell immediately to the Dark Side. She froze, horrified. She had not seen a battle before. The noise, the cries, the clatter and clashing of weapons was a sound like no other. This was destruction at its very worst. The fight for life and death, power and glory was an incomparable force and energy.

Poppy felt the overwhelming fuel of adrenaline pumping through her every vein. The moment came when her 'fight or flight' instinct kicked in. She chose fight and charged and lashed out at any dark creature that came at her. She cried out to Jay to stay with her. The demands on the body to move and manoeuvre through every challenge faced took their toll. Poppy lost focus momentarily and was knocked through the air. She had no idea how, or by what, but her body crashed down, hitting a tree. The blow was, however, softened by the gallant body shield offered by one of Xania's army members. Had it not, she may have faced her doom there and then. Winded, she stood up to see Jay struggling.

She remembered the walking stick Grolban had given her. This could prove helpful. She pulled it out from within her belt. She heard a voice in her mind: *This may offer some use as a protective weapon.* It was the voice of Aviv: 'You must use what you know to protect you, and your gifts and strengths from the human world will be useful here.' Poppy swung her stick hard as if it were a hockey stick. She made contact with a rock. The rock shot up and fired through the air like a comet streaking through the night sky. It struck straight into the centre of a dark creature's soul. The creature turned to dust. Immediately, she realised her power and what she could do. She turned the walking stick so the curved handle was down and swung it, hitting every small rock in sight. She hit another, and another, making contact with target after target. Alfski raced between darting ghastly figures to throw rocks in a bid to assist her. Poppy shouted, 'Jay, use your talents – football, rugby, jumping – Jay, our skills are our power!' Jay, a little cumbersome at first, soon jumped agilely over dark creatures, stumps and branches, arching his back as he performed flips. He dodged dark enemies, kicked and threw rocks at others. In slow motion he was a martial artist, performing the most agile of feints and turns on ground and in air. The forest was a frenzy of activity; Poppy realised what a war zone must be like. The magnitude of the horror, pain and devastation dawned upon her.

She looked briefly up at the sky as the moon and sun drew closer together. The dark army was decreasing in number; this was the time to make her move. She needed to find Xania ... perhaps during the battle the last eggshell piece had been found. Time was running out and with it, the opportunity to fulfil her quest. She took her moment to run for the boundary. Leaping through the invisible barrier she called him. 'Xania! where are you?' Xania bounded around from the rock base but as he did so, a huge shadow of monstrous size stopped him in his tracks. He skidded and jolted sharply back, shooting a glance towards Poppy who was a short distance away. She looked to see what the cause of the distraction could be and froze, paralysed with fear from the sheer size and grotesqueness of the creature.

It must be Vasclaurus. Here he was. Finally, she had come face to face with the evil creature. Her heart beat faster and she suddenly felt scared. She could feel droplets of per-spiration trickle down from her top lip. All that was evil, all that she had ever heard about, was standing in front of her. Standing in her pathway. She felt trapped. The time had finally come. The battle was not over but was about to begin. A battle between her and Vasclaurus. A battle after which one of them would surely live and the other die.

She still had Xania. He could protect her, and there must be a way to defeat this hideous creature between them. Her mind battled with what best to do. The dragonix might just let her run free so he could reign victorious but, then again, he might not. And what would become of Xania and everyone else? Fleeing from Nutash was not an option. She was no coward and therefore was not going to run away. She was not going to give up without a fight and fail all the friends she had made on this incredible journey, many of whom had given up their lives to help her in her quest. She was not going to let them down. No, she owed all of Nutash her bravery.

The beast dropped its head to look at her. He sniffed slowly and studied her, and she held her breath in fear. One shot of flames, she thought, and she would be burned to a cinder. Why was he not doing anything? Why did he not burn her to death there and then? 'Is this what you are looking for ...' he mocked, holding the eggshell piece in his claws. He placed it on the ground carefully just to the side of his mighty talons. His attention then shifted to Jay. 'Ah! The traitor.'

'Be careful, Jay!' Poppy shouted. Vasclaurus drew back a breath and there was a deep-throated rumbling sound. Then a conjured-up ball of fire appeared in his mouth. With an explosive exhalation he hurled it towards Jay who, with his newly sharpened reflexes, leapt high into the air, only just managing to avoid the flickering flames of heat by flipping over backwards. He landed, much to Poppy's relief, with two feet firmly on the ground. Vasclaurus had demonstrated that he could overpower anyone that tried to challenge him. He fired more balls of flame in Jay's direction, and each time Jay narrowly managed to dodge the flames. Poppy wondered how much longer Jay could firedodge for. She saw Vasclaurus looking up to the sky. The sky began to darken, and the sun and moon drew nearer together. Vasclaurus turned his focus away from Jay. He glanced down but jolted back in shock. He looked around in a state of terrified confusion. The eggshell! It was no longer where he had placed it. It had disappeared. Vasclaurus's face was a pool of horror as he skittered about frantically trying to find the piece. He agitated the dirt with his talons. His actions suggested he was filled with overwhelming fear. He would know that the piece could be now on its way to causing his demise. There was fire in his eyes and he looked enraged. He drew back and, it seemed with every ounce of energy within his body, he thrust a stream of fire from his mouth. Poppy fell heavily to the ground as Jay tackled her away from the channel of fire. This only infuriated Vasclaurus further, and he breathed more streaks of fire and clawed at both with his mighty talons.

Alfski appeared. Relief swept over Poppy to know there was further support. He leapt onto Vasclaurus's back and clambered up his neck to his head, clearly distracting the ferocious dragonix from his focus. By now, the moon was very nearly in the shadow of the sun's pathway.

Xania metamorphosed quickly to human form. 'Quick, Poppy! The raspins have taken the three pieces to the summit. You must climb now. Go! Go now! Time is running out. You only have a couple of minutes!'

Poppy started to climb for all her worth. She was an able climber, which aided her speed and judgement. She glanced as Xania metamorphosed back to a wolvern, knowing he could protect her far better this way with his sheer speed and physicality. But in the second Xania took to transform and plant his feet, Vasclaurus swiped him with a mighty blow. The hit sent Xania flying through the air. Poppy knew the only way to put a stop to Vasclaurus and protect her friends from further harm was to climb the mountain and complete the quest.

As she scrambled up the mountainside, she peered behind. Vasclaurus was taking flight and Jay was climbing as quickly as he could, clearly coming to her aid. Like Poppy, Jay's speed was hindered slightly by an occasional slip as crumbling rock gave way underfoot. He then did something either incredibly brave or stupid; he tried to distract Vasclaurus. 'Vasclaurus! Is this what you're looking for?' He pulled off the hessian backpack that had carried the precious eggshell pieces. Vasclaurus diverted his attention from Poppy and landed stealthily on the mountainside looking somewhat confused. The monstrous creature edged steadily down the mountainside. He tugged the backpack from Jay, lifted the flap and sniffed inside. The bag was clearly empty – a clever foil on Jay's part to detain him for a few valuable seconds. Poppy climbed higher as fast as while Vasclaurus was still distracted by Jay, scuffing the rocky soil with his talons enough to send Jay tumbling a short way down the mountain, but not enough to harm him. It was soon clear, however, that Poppy was now his sole target.

Poppy reached the summit. She saw several large rat-like creatures scurrying around – *raspins*. They had placed the three eggshells into the nesting area at the top of the mountain, clearly ready for her to slot together. The moon was nearly in the sun's shadow and the eclipse of the New Blood Moon about to take place. Her heart raced and her stomach filled with nervous energy as she saw Vasclaurus landing next to her. He gazed up at the sun and moon and grinned. 'Oh, such a shame. It is not meant to be, oh little human one, yet you tried so hard. It is now just you and I … and I am afraid this is one battle you will not win.'

Poppy looked around for Xania. He would help her. But where was he? He was nowhere in sight.

'See, they're all gone … it's just you and I …' Vasclaurus jabbed at Poppy's torso with a hooked talon, toying with her. The eclipse was only moments away.

She had not come all this way to be stopped in her tracks when the end of the quest was in her sights. She felt a flame ball of her own, but hers built deep within her soul. The thought of her friends, gone. Her stomach filled with a fireball of anger; furious, she took a strong hold of the walking stick. She paused and looked deep into the eyes of Vasclaurus. She stooped low. She swung the stick back as far as she could, rotating to gain power. Her torso unwound at speed as she reverse-hit a sizable rock she'd spotted in front. The sound of the walking stick making contact with the rock gave her no doubt this was a precision hit. It was a powerful hit like none she had ever struck before. The force and magnitude sent the rock hurtling through the air at a phenomenal pace. The line was perfect. It couldn't have been any more perfect. It struck its target, penetrating deep into Vasclaurus's right eye. The force and pain sent him staggering back. He lost his footing and slid down the mountainside, roaring as he thrashed his head from side to side in agony.

Poppy stumbled back, exhausted from her exertion. She looked up. Did she still have time or was it too late? The moon moved directly into the sun's pathway and the New Blood Moon eclipse was taking place before her very eyes. She made haste to place the pieces of eggshell together, but no! She could not believe it. Where was the third piece? How could this have happened? Not now, surely, when she had risked everything to get to this point and had the pieces. Where was it? She could not believe it. The third piece was missing. She panicked. She looked frantically around. She remembered stepping back on something when she went to swing the stick. It must have been the eggshell piece. She hurled herself to the edge and cried. 'NO!' she screamed, '*no*, please, no!' Tears fell from her eyes. She looked up to the sky as the sun and moon began to meet. She threw herself on the ground and wept. All this for nothing. It was all too late. She had failed. Lives had been lost, for what? The quest was over. She had let everyone down.

Just then she felt something touch her hand. She peered up. Something or someone was pushing the familiar iridescent edge of the dragonix eggshell towards her; it was a human hand. A kind-looking man with a reassuring face appeared. He looked up at the sky and nodded with a sense of urgency.

Poppy rushed to link the three pieces together; frantically, she joined the jagged edges of the eggshell so that they interlocked. She looked around as the ground shook behind her. Vasclaurus was scrambling onto the summit and heading straight her way. He lifted an arm and Poppy looked up as his talons drove down towards her. This was it; she was about to meet her death. But no. It was not to be. The final piece must have sealed just as the mammoth creature was about to strike her down.

Vasclaurus had frozen in time, mid-strike. As with the evil magic of the shop, he too turned slowly ashen then grey. He crumbled steadily and disintegrated to dust, just as the prophecy had said he would. A towering figure that was once an evil and frightening creature crumbled down. Crumbled to nothingness. All that remained was a huge pile of ash. Some fine particles took to the air and blew away in the gentle breeze. There was an atmosphere of calm and serenity and the night was filled with relief and joy. Jay pulled himself up and over the ledge and ran to hug Poppy.

The sky was dark, a clear canvas, brightened by the dotted glistening and twinkling of stars. Then came a most magical light. It was truly radiant. It was the most marvellous light Poppy had ever seen and it was coming from the new egg forming. The egg sparkled, shone and turned lighter in colour. Poppy could see something wonderful, something truly wonderful growing inside. She felt incredibly fortunate to be a part of this remarkably magical moment. The egg's glow began to soften slightly but its beautiful radiating iridescent colours remained. It cracked – just slightly at first; then the cracks became jagged, lengthened and widened as they crept around the egg. It finally broke into three pieces. Poppy and Jay watched on as a stunningly beautiful dragonix grew in size. It evolved before their very eyes. It unfolded, slowly drawing up to a towering height, and it expanded its body and chest, stretching out its far-spanning wings. The new dragonix bore magnificent coloured feathers – tones of pinks, lilacs and golds. As it shook, dust particles shimmered in the moonlit sky. The sight was simply breathtaking.

Distracted, Poppy remembered the rest of the prophecy. She must leave Nutash before the New Blood Moon eclipse ended or she would turn to dust. But where was Xania? She looked away from the new dragonix and raced down the mountainside. Aviv, Ashen, Alfski, the remaining Nutash people and the man who had come to her aid had gathered at the foot of the mountain. Poppy's stomach became a pit of dread. She continued to run down the mountain, followed by Jay, as fast as she could. She prayed she would not find what she feared; the thought that was in the forefront of her mind. Her heart beat wildly and droplets of sweat ran from her face. Her stomach churned. She reached the bottom. There, lying motionless on the ground was Xania.

'Poppy, I'm sorry. He's nearly gone,' said Alfski. 'I'm so very, very sorry.'

Poppy stood like stone. Her eyes filled. 'NO! *No!* He can't be. I won't let him go! No!' She knelt down crying. She hugged and hugged Xania with all her might. She knew she was losing him. She rubbed her hands through his fur and grabbed two handfuls as she pulled her face into him. He lifted his head slightly and looked at her then laid his heavy head back down. His breathing shallowed. Poppy had so much to say. So much to tell him and time was running out. She did not want him to go. She desperately did not want him to leave her. Why did this have to happen? And to Xania? Why? As Xania appeared to draw his last breath, Poppy felt heat from within her pocket. She remembered the timepiece. Could this be of any use at such a time? She took it out and pressed the button. She had two minutes left and she was going to use those final minutes on Xania, her true friend ... a friend she had grown to love dearly.

Time stopped as he lifted his head once more.

'Xania, please don't leave me. You're my friend. I love you. I love you so much. Please don't go. Please, I'm begging you! We've done so much together. We've come so far, so many memories. I don't want you to go, I'll miss you so much. What will I do without you?' she bawled into his fur. It was as if all the unhappiness she had ever experienced, all the sadness about anything she had ever felt, filled her soul. It felt like her very soul was being dragged away from her, was being pulled deep into the ground. Her eyes stung. The deep sadness she experienced had a pain of its own, an emotional pain like no other she had ever endured. Now she knew what it was to have a broken heart. She looked at his limp body and tears fell heavy from her eyes. Saying goodbye and letting go of something she loved was the hardest thing she had ever had to do. It seemed like only seconds had passed; why did time have to go so quickly? The two minutes ended. Everything returned to normal – everything, that was, except Xania, who was now lifeless on the ground. Cold. She put the timepiece down next to him. It served no more purpose.

'I am sorry, but you must hurry, my darling. You've no time to lose,' said Aviv. 'The new dragonix will take you back to the place where you first entered Nutash. Hurry – you must hurry, you've only a minute to spare.' Aviv, Ashen and Alfski hugged Poppy. Quick, rushed farewells just weren't fair. This wasn't the happy ending Poppy was expecting. The new dragonix rose upwards; she flew gently across and picked up Jay, Poppy and the kind stranger delicately with her grand-sized claws. Once secure on her back, she took flight. She covered the land in its entirety swiftly and easily. It took only seconds to reach the hole in the ground where they had first entered Nutash. Poppy scrambled through first, closely followed by Jay and finally the man. Poppy turned to look back. At that very moment, there was a flash of colour that could be seen at the entrance of the hole. Dirt fell in and with it, the entrance closed. They were all back. Back in Tuckenhay.

Chapter 11
Tuckenhay

The gentleman knelt up on one knee. He brushed the soil from his trouser legs and shirt and looked towards Poppy and Jay. They had all been through quite an ordeal so Poppy took a moment to internalise and digest her thoughts and feelings. She looked at the pleasant-faced gentleman. He had mousey brown hair that receded at the temples and he seemed to be of a kind disposition. He smiled a gentle smile and appeared to be waiting for Poppy to speak first. Poppy tried to rationalise her thoughts. 'Sorry … how did you … how do you know about …?'

The gentleman pre-empted the question and interjected. 'I know about Nutash,' he said. 'I went there once myself. Like you, I found this place, stumbled upon it purely by accident. I was not much older than the two of you. I was not as special as you, however, Poppy. The wolvern you befriended clearly felt you had the tenacity to save his land. I suppose I knew this time would come, but the hustle and bustle of daily life often distracted my thoughts from the magical place I once knew. I suppose at times I questioned my own sanity, thinking that finding Nutash must have been just a dream. When I heard about two children going missing in this area, I had a suspicion, a sort of intuitive knowing, I guess. My hunches are not often wrong. Most helpful with my line of work, I must add. I'm a police inspector, by the way. I work at Tuckenhay Police Station, just down the road from here. Oh – apologies! I haven't introduced myself yet. I'm Inspector Mike Waghorn.' He held out his hand to shake.

'Does anyone else know about Nutash. Did you tell anyone?' asked Poppy.

'Oh, no, no,' said Inspector Waghorn. 'I'm not sure they would have believed me. Do you? I'm hoping for a promotion. It's been a long time coming. Now if I were to go into my office and tell my super I'd found a magic land, he'd think I'd lost my marbles! And the only thing I'd be finding then is a new job! That wouldn't do, would it?'

'But we could show them,' said Jay. 'Then they'd have to believe us.'

'We could, but as with other magical places in life, I imagine, you can only visit them when the time is right, when the magic deems it is time for you to go there. That's the wonder of such places,' said Inspector Waghorn. 'How would it be if you did tell people about the land and you brought the two worlds together? How would that be for the inhabitants of Nutash? Would they really fit in this world? No. Magic is about mystery. You bring worlds together and the mystery is gone.

'Poppy, this is our special secret then. It's a good secret. It's what we would call a safe secret, so we won't tell anyone. It is just something we will know about and carry with us, just like the inspector has. Maybe one day we could tell our children or grandchildren about Nutash.'

Poppy nodded.

Inspector Mike Waghorn talked to them for some time about his visit to Nutash while the children sat in the sunshine listening intently. Intrigued and fascinated, they had many questions.

'How did you get into Nutash?' asked Poppy.

'The same way as you I imagine, by the river? I saw footprints there, or rather my colleague spotted them first. So that's how I knew you were there. That's how I first entered Nutash as a boy. I was playing along the river and I saw a very interesting looking tree. I sat in the alcove admiring the roots and then I saw a strange light.'

'That's exactly what happened to us!' said Jay.

'And Aviv and Ashen?' asked Poppy.

'Oh yes, dear old Aviv and Ashen. Such a lovely couple, it was quite a surprise for them I'd imagine when I turned up at their door. I'm sure I was the last person they were expecting to see. Still, we had time to have a quick catch up over a saphberry brew before coming to find you two.'

'Well …' said the inspector after a while. 'It's high time I got you back to your mother. She will no doubt be incredibly worried as to your whereabouts.'

'What will we tell her?' Poppy asked. 'She might be cross if we don't have a good explanation as to where we've been.'

'I know what to say,' said Inspector Waghorn. 'I will just explain that you deviated from your track and got lost, so you bedded down for the night and I found you in the morning. I am sure your mother will be relieved to know you're both fit and well. That way, I'm not being dishonest, I'm just being economical with all with the information I give.' The children agreed.

'But the time!' said Poppy. 'We've been gone for days. Mum will wonder what we've been doing and why we couldn't find our way back or ask someone.'

'You have only been missing less than 24 hours. The passage of time in this world and of the one you have just come from are very different,' said Inspector Waghorn.

This made Poppy feel better.

As they walked back, Poppy noticed that everything in Tuckenhay was just as they had left it. The meadow looked inviting with its tall grass and sprinkling of colourful wild flowers. The weather remained gloriously sunny and warm and the sky was blue with the occasional stationary fluffy white cloud. Poppy and Jay noted Billy and Elsie the goats grazing leisurely. 'Look, your girlfriend's still there!' Poppy said.

'Yeah, but notice how yours turned away when he saw you!'

It seemed like normality was returning once again between the pair. The events of before were now becoming a distant memory.

When Poppy arrived at the cottage with Jay and the inspector, her mum was elated. She was overwhelmed with happiness to see both children returned safe and sound. She made the inspector a cup of tea while he provided an explanation for the disappearances. She hugged the Poppy and Jay and thanked the inspector between making phone calls to let family members know that all was well. Once Inspector Waghorn had said goodbye and left, Mrs Raleigh suggested the children take it in turns to have a shower. 'You must feel terribly uncomfortable having had a rough night. Once you've showered and changed, I'm sure you will feel refreshed and ready for lunch. You must be awfully hungry, you poor things.'

As Poppy made her way to the bathroom she turned her focus to Dudley. He had made such a big fuss of her when she returned. He had settled himself and was lying by the kitchen door following her every move with his chocolate brown eyes as if worried she would leave him again. She knelt down and hugged him and kissed him gently on his nose. She rubbed his fleecy coat grabbing tufts of fur as she buried her face into his neck. At that moment, a vision came into her mind, and then a feeling of sadness; her mind became distracted as she thought of Xania.

Chapter 12
The Blood Moon

As the days passed Poppy often thought about Xania. The aching she felt in her heart, at times, was quite difficult to bear. She understood that this was a natural response to losing something you loved. There were periods between the fun holiday activities when she would become distracted and think of him. It was the quiet times where her subconscious thoughts ran wild and memories infiltrated her mind. Poppy knew that talking to someone you trusted was a good thing to do if you felt sad or upset. Thankfully, she had Jay. Jay would often offer helpful advice or distract any melancholy moments with jokes and laughter. He was a real source of support over the days that followed, and he managed to make her feel much happier as they filled their time with normal activities.

'We need to get an early start tomorrow, you two,' said Mrs Raleigh. 'So I would pack your things now if I were you, then make the most of the beautiful weather on your last day. I have said that we won't be having a late night tonight, but the villagers are having a barbeque this evening out on the green to celebrate the Blood Moon eclipse that's occurring in the early hours of the morning, for those wanting to stay up to see it, that is. And that will not include you two, I'm afraid to say!' Poppy and Jay looked at each other with disappointment.

'What is a Blood Moon eclipse?' asked Jay.

'Well … I'm not a scientist, Jay, but I think it's something to do with the reflection of light. If my memory of physics serves me correctly, the moon reflects light from the sun. When the earth moves between the sun and moon in a total eclipse, it cuts off the light reflected pathway. Rather than the moon going dark, it goes a reddish colour. That's what I understand it to be, but don't take my word for it. I may be wrong. Perhaps you might like to do a little research of your own. You could enlighten me if I have incorrectly informed you.' The thought of doing any work-related research was not something that filled Jay with enthusiasm so he decided packing would be a far better option, followed by the prospect of enticing Poppy into a tennis rematch once finished.

When packed, the children went out to the tennis court. They had an exciting final game. The match was close, and, much to Jay's delight, he managed to beat Poppy on match point. After the game, they took their rackets back to the cottage. They ambled along, a little tired from their exertion. Mrs Raleigh had prepared a hearty lunch as usual and, once finished, Poppy and Jay decided to take Dudley for one final long walk. They went to the meadow and said their goodbyes to Billy and Elsie, the goats. Taking in all their wonderful surroundings, they acknowledged the place that had offered such a wonderful adventure. An adventure more unbelievable and magical than they could have ever thought possible. Teatime drew nearer and Jay and Poppy headed home to get ready for the barbeque. They walked a large loop around the village to ensure they had encompassed all of Tuckenhay before leaving. An occasional car went by, and then a police car. It was Inspector Waghorn. He waved to both of them. 'He didn't stop,' said Poppy. 'We could have said goodbye. He won't know we're going tomorrow. That's such a shame. I wanted to say goodbye again.'

'He's probably going to sort something out. He'll be on his way somewhere. He's on duty, so I doubt he could find time to stop. Perhaps he'll be at the barbeque later.'

The children went home and got ready for the evening. 'What's going to happen at the barbeque?' said Poppy.

'Well, there will be food, obviously,' said Mrs Raleigh. 'Apparently there will be live music too. I am sure there'll be lots of other children to play with.'

'Play with! We're not babies,' said Poppy.

'Well, socialise with then. You know what I mean. And that will be enough of that sarcasm, young lady, if you don't mind.'

'Sor-ry!' said Poppy. 'Can we take Dudley?'

'I'd rather not,' said Mrs Raleigh. 'He might prove bothersome.'

'Oh. We'd take good care of him, I promise. Please! Please, Mum.'

'We will, Mrs Raleigh. We promise. We will.'

'Well ... alright, but if he proves a nuisance, he'll have to come home. Is that quite clear?'

Mrs Raleigh locked the door to the cottage while Poppy and Jay fussed over Dudley. As they descended the cascading stone steps they saw the hazy grey smoke from the barbeque, followed by the most glorious smell of food. The smell was enough to entice anyone's hunger to sample the delights on offer. By the time they reached the green, the barbeque was in full flow. Mrs Raleigh was greeted by some neighbouring holidaymakers. Poppy and Jay went off to explore. The music was lively and there was a jolly atmosphere. Holidaymakers and locals alike were engaged in conversation, eating and drinking. Poppy took in the coloured bunting around the green, the contagious beat of the rhythm from the band as she absorbed all the merriment taking place. Then in the distance, she saw the inspector. Inspector Waghorn was there. Poppy and Jay ran across to him and spent a little time talking, pleased to be able to say one final goodbye. As dusk fell, the atmosphere and ambience continued with the turning on of fairy lights, which all added to the enchantment.

Poppy's mum came to say that it was nearly bedtime and that the children had five more minutes. 'Where's Dudley?'

Poppy and Jay realised Dudley was no longer with them. 'He was here a moment ago because I fed him a piece of burger,' Poppy said. 'I'll find him, don't worry. He can't be far. Stay there, Jay, and I'll go. If I can't find him I'll let you know, Mum.'

'Right. Well, don't be too long. If he doesn't surface in a few minutes, come and find me. Don't go too far away, will you?'

'No, I won't.' Jay remained with some new friends he had made while Poppy went to look for Dudley.

Poppy initially looked in the immediate vicinity. There was no obvious sign of Dudley. *He must have found a scent of an animal or something,* she thought. *Trust him to go off and let me down when I fought his corner to come here.*

Night had fallen now. The sky was a deep shade of blue and lit with the brightest and whitest of stars. Not a cloud was in sight. The moon was fully exposed. It appeared larger and rounder than usual and it was the most stunning orange colour. It was perfect. Poppy couldn't see any imperfections no matter how hard she studied to find some. She wondered whether the moon phases were all equally beautiful. Was she so preoccupied with life that she never took time to notice the simple wonders and magic on her own doorstep? The moon appeared to be waiting. It was like the start of a theatre show when the lights go down and all the chatter fades, then the anticipation, the pause before the entertainment. The moon was waiting for its entertainment – its eclipse. As Poppy walked further away from the green the sounds of chatter, laughter and music seeped gently into the distance. But where was the entertainment?

All was calm, quiet, tranquil. Dudley was the entertainment. 'Dudley! Dudley! Stupid dog, where are you?' There was no response ... no sound or indication that Dudley was anywhere in the area.

Poppy thought she heard what sounded like a howl. She couldn't remember a time when she had been out in the dark of night alone. She knew of different nocturnal animals and that foxes had peculiar calls, but she had no idea what animal would make this one. It sounded like a wolf, but sense prevailed she knew they did not exist in these parts. She heard a rustling sound. She stopped. She looked and peered, her eyes squinting slightly to focus; there, from out of the woody area, came something small and blonde in colour, growling. Dudley! It was Dudley. At last.

Relieved, Poppy called to him. 'Dudley! Come here, you stupid animal! What have you been doing and what is it you've found? A fox? You silly thing!' Dudley raced over and jumped up and down on his hind legs then started to walk back to the woody area, but he hesitated and growled.

'Come here,' said Poppy. 'Do as you're told.' She looked on, curious, as she heard further rustling. 'It's just a stupid fox, now come here and let's get back.' But Dudley was steadfast in his determination to stay fixed to the spot. Poppy looked harder. The rustling noise was far louder than anything a single fox could create. She was a little worried at that point; she thought about running back and hoped Dudley would follow quickly. She took a few steps back, more concerned now about what was only metres away from her. There was a moment of quiet, of calm, a strange eeriness. Then something started pushing through the bushes. From the movement of the foliage, it was an animal of size. Poppy knew immediately this was not a stag or deer; it wouldn't be brave enough to come towards a growling dog or watching human for that matter. This was something wild, possibly predatory. She stepped back as the animal appeared from out of the wood. Its shape and outline were oddly familiar. It had the physical appearance of a bear or a wolf. She stopped. Her heart raced. As it walked into the moonlight she could see it clearer. Its coat was a pinkie-violet colour. It couldn't be. Were her eyes deceiving her? Could it be? Could it really be? Xania. Her heart beat faster and excitement filled her stomach. She walked forward. The animal did not fear her. It did not run away. 'Xania! Is that you?'

The animal walked forward. The corners of its mouth seemed to turn upwards as if smiling. 'Yes, it is.'

'You can speak!'

'Well, I am in your world now.'

'But … but you were dead. You died in front of me.'

'I would have. But you saved me.'

'How? How come?'

'Well … you see, Nutash is a very special place. Do you remember what Aviv said to you? "A friendship made in Nutash lives forever …" Well, I guess we must have a very special friendship.' Seeing Xania was like all the best gifts ever bottled and consumed. She felt warm inside. Complete. She flung her arms around his neck and hugged him tightly. He nestled his nose deep into the nape of her neck. There they stayed. Butterflies darted within her stomach and tears of joy rolled down her cheeks. Xania moved his head to look at her. He licked the salty droplets from her face; she laughed and, grabbing his face, pulled him towards her and kissed his dark wet nose. Then came a voice.

'Poppy! Poppy! Where are you?'

Poppy heard her mum calling her.

'I must go,' Xania said.

'Don't. Please don't leave me. Not again.'

'I must, Poppy. I cannot exist here in your world. You know this.'

'But I could hide you. There must be a way!'

'There is no way. Quickly, there is no time to lose. I have this for you.' Xania fumbled with his teeth for a moment then pulled something out of the hessian backpack strapped around his body. 'Here. You left this.'

'What is it?' she asked. She looked more closely. It was the timepiece.

'It has been adjusted by Grolban,' said Xania.

Poppy could hear her mum's voice louder. She was no longer in the distance but heading right her way and was now in full sight. Poppy took the timepiece.

'I must go,' said Xania. With that, he ran towards the wooded area near the river alcove where Poppy and Jay had first entered Nutash.

Poppy shouted out, 'But what do I do with this … ?'

'Poppy, what are you doing down there? Who are you talking to?'

Xania turned. 'You'll know … you'll know when the time is right …'

Poppy watched. She turned sharply round to look at her mother walking down the bank then quickly returned her gaze to watch Xania. She looked longingly as he swiftly navigated the terrain, his body stealthily twisting and turning with the undulating course of his path. He was nearly out of view. He paused and turned to look at her once more. Their eyes locked. Poppy half lifted her hand to wave. He turned and disappeared into the wood – gone, completely out of sight. Poppy stood feeling bewildered and confused.

'What are you doing down here all on your own? Who were you talking to?'

Poppy clutched the timepiece and angled her body slightly so she could slip it into her pocket without her mum seeing; she wanted to avoid any awkward questions. 'I was talking to Dudley. He's here. He'd found a fox.'

As she walked back up the bank with her mum, she moved her hand discreetly behind and fumbled gently in her back pocket to feel the timepiece once more. She wanted reassurance it was there. What did Xania mean when he said she would know when to use it? What was she to do? She wished she had had longer with him before they were prematurely interrupted, but at least he was alive. Even though he was not with her, to think he would be back living with Aviv and Ashen in Nutash was so reassuring. She couldn't wait to tell Jay what had happened.

'Well, I expect poor Jay will probably wonder where we've got to.'

'Yeah, I feel bad just leaving him there all this time without me.'

'Come here, my lovely girl, I can see you're shivering. Let me put my arm around you to warm you up. There. How's that?'

'Much better,' said Poppy.

'So, can I ask, have you had a good time in Tuckenhay? Has it been a good holiday?'

'Yes, Mum, I have. It's been great. And Mum, I love you so much. Thank you.'

Poppy walked up the hill cuddling into her mum. She breathed in the night air and let out a gentle sigh. Then she lifted her head and gazed up at the clear night sky, and as she did so she could see the sun and moon drawing nearer together. She smiled. A warming glow of contentment filled her inside, and she knew everything was going to be just fine.